A Dangerous Freedom

The Divided America Zombie Apocalypse

Book Three

B. D. Lutz

ACKNOWLEDGEMENTS

Edited by Monique Happy Editorial Services
www.moniquehappyeditorial.com

Thank you for your hard work and guidance. But most of all, thank you for answering a random email from a newbie.

Cover designed by: Kelly A. Martin
www.kam.design

Kelly, you are a master at your craft!

Photography by chagpg (DepositPhotos), Nik_Merkulov (DepositPhotos), chagpg (DepositPhotos), vzmaze (DepositPhotos), Josh Lin (Scopio), guvendemir (iStock)

Prologue

First Vice Chair Choke sat quietly, reviewing the Proclamation from Dear Leader in one hand and the picture of it being signed by Dear Leader in the other. His head pivoted between the two; his disbelief at what his eyes told him was all-consuming. *This cannot be. I should be DPRK Supreme Leader in Dear Leader's absence. It is my rightful duty.*

With the failure of his weapon and the rise of his treacherous political adversary, his sanity was slipping away. He would soon lose his life if he failed to wrench control away from Packet.

Vice Chair Packet snatched the phone from Choke's grasp. "Enough! The information will not change to fit your wishes." Packet breathed in the power he held and continued, "Dear Leader demanded we begin planning to invade America. The DPRK no longer views our pact with the Coalition as valid. All the land is ours to take, and we will start our offensive soonest!"

Choke stood and locked Packet in a hard stare. The leathery little serpent should be dead, killed by anti-aircraft guns, then fed to starving dogs. He'd witnessed the anger in Dear Leader's eyes only hours ago in this very room. Anger that assured Choke of Packet's execution.

"VC Packet. I have many questions regarding this transfer of power."

Packet moved in close to Choke as he spoke. Not intimidated, Choke countered the move with a hard step in Packet's direction.

A muffled thump, emanating from Dear Leader's private quarters, interrupted their standoff. Packet appeared rattled by the sound, and Choke pounced on the show of weakness.

With narrowed eyes, he made a show of slowly glancing to the door of Dear Leader's private quarters, then to Packet. "Packet, who occupies Dear Leader's glorious space?"

"You will refer to me as Supreme Leader Packet. Furthermore, not only have I taken leadership of the DPRK, I inherited the pleasantries that accompany my position. She is but twenty-one and untouched until now. Probably just recovering from our time together."

An unbelieving grunt preceded Choke's words. "I will not honor you with the title of Supreme Leader. You are a fraud, Packet. A fraud who will be executed by flame-thrower after I expose you. Although, considering the brief time that passed from your call until I entered this room, you probably were with a woman."

Ignoring the insult, Packet aimed to defang the snake in front of him. "Tell me, Choke. Why are DPRK citizens tearing each other apart in the streets? What monster did you unleash upon our country?"

Another, more forceful, thump shook the door to Dear Leader's quarters, prompting Packet to move into a position meant to block Choke's access to the private quarters. The move did not escape Choke; he was done with the petty little man claiming to be the anointed one. Choke rushed past Packet and flung open the door. The wall of stench that collided with Choke's senses overpowered him. The sight of Dear Leader hogtied on the floor, wallowing in his own foulness, brought him to his knees as he retched and heaved his stomach's contents to the marble floor.

No longer burdened by the charade, Packet burst into maniacal laughter at the sight of the mighty First Chairman on his knees. He approached the pathetic man and delivered a vicious blow to the back of his head. "Let me help you get it all out. Such a weak little toad you are." Grabbing a fistful of the dazed Choke's hair, he forced his head up and screamed, "Look at what you've created, at what you did to our Dear Leader. Our beautiful DPRK is transforming into this atrocity as we speak! You should have listened to me!"

"No, this is not possible. What did you do, Packet? How did this happen?"

"Dear Leader is … I'm sorry, *was* nothing more than a dope head. Just like the ones you infected on the streets of America!" Rage overtaking him, Packet slammed Choke's head against the doorframe, nearly rendering him unconscious and opening a large, ragged gash on his fleshy forehead.

Packet shook Choke violently and screamed, "You stay awake and enjoy the view of the world you have created as our streets run red with the blood of our people."

With a sharp thrust he released Choke's hair, retrieved Dear Leader's sat-phone, and selected the number of the slimy dotard, Senator Shafter. As his finger hovered over the send button, the phone buzzed to life.

In heavily accented English, Packet answered. "Ah, your fragile little back could not bear the burden of not speaking to Dear Leader. Dear Leader is not willing to speak to imperialist scum. What do you desire, Senator Worm?"

"What do I desire? You arrogant little prick, put Kim on the line. The Coalition *desires* answers."

"I already tell you, Dear Leader has no time for worm. I speak for him. Talk or I hang up."

After a stunned pause, Shafter asked, "What is happening on our streets? Your weapon seems out of control. Why are people eating one another? What have you done?" Shafter was now screaming through the tiny speaker, bringing a perverse amusement to Packet. "A week hasn't even passed and your monsters are running crazed in our streets. We cannot hide this much longer. We live in the social media age; everyone outside of the DPRK owns a phone with a camera."

Packet spat, "You shut you face, you maggot. DPRK cannot help that your streets are full of dope heads. Maybe the blood of inferior Americans not mixes well with the superior chemicals DPRK's most prestigious scientists used. Don't you worry, we have the cure. Tell Senators Stretch Face and Fecal-stein you get what you ask for. Dear Leader see you soon." Packet broke into uncontrollable laughter as he ended the call with the screaming senator.

Choke sprang from the floor and slammed the door on the horrible reality of his failure. His blood-soaked vision hid Packet from sight as he searched the room for the man. Resorting to following the sound of Packet's cackling, he lowered his head and thrust out his arms while charging the area where the depraved man should be standing. His hands made contact, then his arms crumpled as he plowed headlong into the column Packet had positioned himself in front of, moving just as Choke arrived.

The last thing he remembered as he lost his battle to remain conscious was Packet's voice. "You need to move faster to catch me. Rest well, little man, our plan to force the imperialist scum to their knees begins when you wake."

Chapter 1
Bobby Smith

"BSU soldiers stationed in RAM. This is Lieutenant Williams. Cease hostilities and remain at your current location. EVAC orders to follow. I repeat, cease hostilities and await further instructions. Williams, out."

During his three weeks in captivity, this was the first time the routine had changed. He welcomed the deviation, even if it meant death for his troops.

"LT, this is Smith, squad call sign OMI 2. We will not stand down. Mission will continue as planned. We have sacrificed too much. Our people have died supporting this effort. RAM has our blood on its hands. You're a coward. Smith, out."

Williams regarded Albright through swollen, blood-crusted eyes. "That was Bobby Smith. He's a former Protection Club leader and the only true fighter in any of my squads. If not for some physical limitations, he could have been regular Army before the virus hit. I didn't put him in charge of field operations because of what you just heard; he's unpredictable and has authority issues. He elevated BSU's hatred of RAM to unprecedented levels. My guess is that he will move to secure supplies, recruit others, and launch a guerrilla warfare campaign against RAM outposts."

Albright swallowed the urge to pummel Williams and radio Smith to advise him he'd soon be dead. But it was imperative he remain silent or the plan to keep BSU units in place for easy termination would fall apart. RAM couldn't allow them to scatter like trash blowing in the street. Willis, FST1, and the other units were already en route to engage the BSU units. He estimated the strike force needed another twenty minutes to eliminate the threats.

"Tell me about Smith. What winds his clock, what's his location, his level of training, and why didn't you identify him before? If he kills one of my people, you'll beg me to end you."

Williams' vision swam. He had just given an order that would kill his troops. Slaughter them. He wanted out, NOW. "Violence towards conservatives, West 220th and Westwood Road, exceptional training, and I didn't know if he was still alive."

"Let's recap. Then we determine your fate. Give me the details one more time."

Williams' exhaustion consumed him. He considered attacking Albright to force the man to kill him. Head heavy and facing the tabletop, he went through the information for the umpteenth time. "Tugs from North Point Marina, Illinois transport cargo to Racine, Wisconsin. They were still operating when RAM sanitized Port Buffalo. The operation in La Bartolina, Mexico using Carretera Matamoros–

Playa Bagdad for Gulf access to Brazos Island State Park in Texas dumped thousands of monsters before it went dark early in the operation."

Williams paused for a sip of water, trying to wash a pasty film from his mouth. "We breached RAM's wall between Nevada and Utah near the Dixie National Forest. It's the perfect location; remote, untouched, and heavily wooded. The forest provided cover from drones, and the landscape is too rugged for regular foot patrols. BSU set up a camp in a secluded town called Caliente, Nevada. The dead get trucked from Las Vegas, loaded into holding pens, herded onto military transports, and carried to within two miles of the breach. At one point, BSU soldiers were using live civilians from the town as bait. They chained people to the wall. Their screams attracted the dead to the breach. When it became too hazardous for the soldiers to approach the wall, they stopped. It didn't matter; they had created a current of dead flowing towards the breach."

Albright was reviewing his notes as Williams spoke, looking for the slightest variation in his narrative. So far, he was verbatim in his telling.

Noticing that Williams had stopped talking, Albright addressed him. "How big is the breach?"

Sighing in frustration, Williams said, "I don't know for sure, but I recall Shafter expressing his displeasure with the outcome." After a lengthy silence, he said, "I have something to add." Albright locked eyes with the physical wreck of a man. "The fact that our West 117th Street operation didn't respond to my announcement is a problem."

Albright recognized what Williams meant; he shot to his feet and grabbed his radio. "Albright for Willis. How copy."

He received only static in reply.

Chapter 2
Dangerous Idiots

Willis had taken cover behind one of their two Humvees, its turreted, .50 caliber gun trained on the small dollar store's west-facing entrance. It felt good knowing that Ma Deuce had their six today. He wished he knew Andrews, the soldier on Ma's trigger, better. But he was assured he was a capable soldier. *You better be right about him, Albright!*

During his mission briefing, Albright had identified this building as the BSU-HQ for Operation Move In, but it hadn't shown any activity, inside or out, since they arrived. The absence of military men and machines put Willis on edge.

With three new soldiers assigned to his squad and no sign they had identified the correct location, Willis clicked off everything that could bounce sideways. But one stood out amongst the rest: Ambush!

"Lewis for Sergeant Willis, how copy?"

"Good copy for Willis. Talk to me, Lewis."

Lewis was in an overwatch position atop a gas station canopy, to the north of the building. The position afforded him a lengthwise view of the entire store and a sightline of the structure's only window.

"They blocked the windows with shelving units and coolers, leaving a small gap for viewing. I can confirm that I see no lights on, over."

Chewing on the information for a moment, Willis decided to enter the store. Whoever occupied this building should know of their presence, meaning they've opted to fight.

Retrieving the bullhorn from the Hummer, Willis addressed their unseen enemy. "This is Sergeant Willis, RAM Army. You are surrounded. Exit with your hands over your head. This is your only warning."

Thirty seconds later, Willis gave the command to enter the building. Like a well-oiled machine, his squad stacked at the entrance, destroyed the door with the breaching ram, deployed a flash bang, and followed Willis into the dark, musty, building. Weapon-mounted flashlights sliced through the dim interior as they paired into two-man teams and searched the store's confines.

"Clear!" Stevenson yelled from the back room as Willis called it for the front of the store.

Stevenson continued, "Three bodies in front of the fire exit. All with multiple gunshot wounds to their backs. Sergeant, you need to see this."

Willis rushed to Stevenson's location and found him crouched, examining bloody footprints on the linoleum near the loading dock.

"A lot of activity took place after those BSU soldiers were executed."

"How so, Stevenson?" Willis asked.

"We have multiple sets of boots tracking blood away from the bodies, none moving towards the bodies."

"Still not following you, Stevenson."

"Look around. The gun locker was forced open, and empty food packages are scattered all over. Everything of value you'd expect to find in this place is missing. Whatever happened here was violent and fast." He paused and glanced up, meeting Willis' stare. "Did you find any spent brass while clearing the building?"

Willis pondered the question. "Not one."

Stevenson stood and met the eyes of each squad member. "This is how it happened. Another group of BSU soldiers arrived and gained access without question. A fight over supplies ensued. Outgunned, these three attempted to escape and were executed. The Army-issue boot treads indicate the killers were all soldiers. Ammo, food, guns, anything of value, was taken."

Willis took in the scene. Stevenson had nailed it. "It also tells us that some of these idiots are still dangerous." The realization hit Willis hard. "Shit! Somebody get FST1 on the radio, NOW!"

Chapter 3
Redoubt

The final section of cyclone fence was being strung and reinforced, while the undersized backhoe, scavenged from a drainage supply company, dropped its last bucketful of earth into the rammed-earth formworks. Dillan never imagined being a history buff would be useful, in a practical sense, until today. But the knowledge he had gained through years of studying ancient cultures brought him to the finished structure now protecting his home.

The idea for the rammed-earth fortification was born from necessity. Before construction began, they determined that the additional cyclone fencing, secured from Jay's construction yard, wasn't enough to enclose the entire community. When the challenge presented itself, he realized that the dirt excavated from the pit-traps they'd planned could fill the gaps.

History reminded him that rammed-earth had been used for thousands of years to build barriers. Using the original sections of the Great Wall of China as inspiration, Dillan organized runs for the needed supplies, organized the construction teams, and started the back-breaking work.

For over three weeks, they fended off attacks from UC hordes, improvised when supplies ran low, and overcame equipment failures. To put it in military terms, *they adapted and overcame.*

Every member of the community worked on the construction team either full-time or between shifts of other assigned tasks. Even Otto served his time. Although listening to Otto talk, he simultaneously enjoyed the work and compared it to chain gang labor. He also seemed to forget that he'd poked the government in the proverbial eye, cutting the community off from supplies they needed during the construction of the desperately needed barrier. He'd only just recently relented and agreed to the mission FST1 was conducting at this very minute.

How'd that go? "I hereby declare this community an independent state. He really is a crazy SOB," Dillan mused aloud. "I hope they're safe," he muttered while watching the tampers mount the formworks and start the tooth-rattling job of packing the earth into what would become the wall.

"What's that, Dillan?" Jay asked.

"Oh, just thinking about FST1 and crossing my fingers they don't end up in another situation like Terra Alta."

Jay chuckled and nodded his agreement. "Otto really is crazy. I'm sure they have it under control. Don't forget, Lisa's with them; she'll keep them safe. Hey, think she'll punch Otto again?"

It was Dillan's turn to laugh. "That's true, Jay. And if Otto can keep his mouth shut, she won't dot-his-eye again. So, knowing Otto, chances are good that he'll have a tattoo of Lisa's knuckles on his face when they get back."

Still laughing, Dillan returned to his diagrams, reviewing them for the thousandth time. The barrier was laid out in a five-pointed star pattern. At six feet high, the rammed-earth walls, topped with four-inch-long spikes, formed the tip of each point with raised guard platforms, similar to catwalks, positioned just behind the wall. They extended towards the community for fifty yards on both sides. At fifty yards, the cyclone fence stretched for another forty yards. Abandoned homes outside the community had been boarded up and became part of the wall. Trenches four foot wide by four foot deep were dug in front of the cyclone fencing turning the six-foot-high fence into an unclimbable ten-foot-high obstacle.

The star pattern should funnel an invading force, living or dead, to the area where the stars' individual points (or twinklers as Otto called them) met. As the enemy was herded along the wall, they would encounter various obstacles including landscaping boulders, ankle-high tripwires, and hundreds of punji sticks waiting to impale them after the tripwire sent them crashing to the ground. He remained frustrated by the lack of progress getting the drones airborne. Both were controlled via, now obsolete, cell phone apps. Nonetheless, the seed was sown and they continued to work towards adding them to their defenses.

If the enemy navigated those obstacles, they would plummet into the pits where additional punji awaited their arrival. The fencing also enabled the community to use pikes, placed through the fencing, to eliminate any threats standing in front of them. With the way UCs massed together, the danger of a trench filling up, enabling other UCs to use their brethren's twisted carcasses as a platform, was real. That danger dictated that the pikes be ten to fifteen feet long, enabling them to kill any threat before it reached the trenches.

The original raised platform guard towers remained in their current locations, offering a comprehensive view of the area surrounding the camp. Dillan took in their accomplishment and decided a vacation day was in order. *We'll start on the early warning system next week.*

His radio burst to life, snapping his deliberation. "South wall for Dillan."

"Go for Dillan."

"You need to see this. You won't believe me otherwise."

Chapter 4
Timmy Trenchant

"Willis for FST1. Your INTEL is bad. The enemy is armed and dangerous."

"Well, no shit, Willis. We figured that out when bullets started flying in our direction!"

"Otto, did FST1 take any casualties, over?"

"Willis, we would need to be able to move from cover to get shot. But we're pinned down. The best we can do is take wild shots over the hood of our Hummer. That reminds me, we need a replacement Hummer. Ours is full of holes."

"Can you flank them? Or set Randy up to snipe them?"

"Why Randy? I'm an excellent shot, too. That's just insulting, Willis. Or should I say, *Timmy Trenchant?*"

"Well, smartass, what's your strategy? Throwing rocks? Wait, I bet you'll use some fancy trick from Hogan's Heroes?" He continued, "Timmy *Trenchant?* Did you get a word of the day calendar for Christmas?"

"Willis, you are so far down my list—."

Willis cut me off. "I know, I know, Otto. I'm so far down your list I'm now on the list of people you don't like.

Well, that's a crowded list. But not nearly as crowded as the *I don't like Otto* list."

The truth in Willis' childish retort stung, but only a little. Because, well, it was true.

"Whatever, Willis! And no, throwing rocks isn't our strategy. We'll talk about my ideas from Hogan's Heroes later. Our plan is to let them shoot at us until they run out of ammo. Because, and you'll love this part, we are PINNED DOWN!"

"Otto, hold tight, we're on our way. ETA twenty minutes. Willis, out."

"Hey, don't rush yourselves. Oh, a bunch of UCs joined the party. So there's that." Willis didn't respond. *Nice. Just abandon us, jerk!*

As round after round ricocheted off the Hummer, I grew more and more angry that it had happened again. We were under siege by people trying to kill us because of bad military INTEL.

Lisa and Stone had already crossed the street and reached the door of the two-story house when shots started flying from two second-story windows. They were now hunkered down under a bench next to the door.

If the idiots—who'd proved to be heavily armed—figured out Lisa and Stone's location, they'd slaughter them. Well, not today, jackasses!

On the plus side, they were in a better position to defend our flank from the UCs who had just joined the party.

We coordinated our return fire at the people attempting to exterminate us, with Lisa and Stone's as they fired on the UCs approaching our left flank. We hoped it would drown out their shots, keeping them hidden from the BSU soldiers in the house.

The Hummer's angle blocked our view of the monsters flanking us from the left. And if Lisa and Stone hadn't noticed them, Randy and I would be dead, or undead, depending on how hungry the UCs were. We coordinated our fire with hand signals from Stone. I laid flat on my belly and watched him from under the Hummer. When he raised his fist, Randy and I would hoist our weapons over the hood of the Hummer and shoot, one-handed, in the general direction of the windows.

That the window shooters increased their barrage every time we shot at them meant we were only pissing them off. Not to mention, we weren't hitting anything but some unlucky bird nests stuffed in the home's gutters. With the SAW trapped in the Hummer, and no clear shots at the windows, we were in a hopeless standoff.

"Randy, why isn't Will here?"

"He was training a group of kids on self defense tactics. Oh, and we have worthless mission INTEL. These idiots were supposed to be unarmed and harmless."

"Huh. Sure would be nice to have one more person pinned down with us."

Stone raised his fist and I moved to shoot at the window, followed by Randy. Ten shots later, Stone had neutralized the threat.

"We can't do this forever; eventually, those idiots will figure us out. The fact that they haven't tried to flank us is dumbfounding."

"Listen to you. Otto the strategist."

"Wouldn't that be a tactic?"

"Really, Otto, now is the time you want to argue military terminology? I was giving you a compliment."

"Oh, in that case, please accept my apology, Randy. I'm not used to compliments from you."

Stone raised his hand, prompting us into another round of random shots. The return fire from the window increased dramatically and didn't end.

Randy crunched into a tight ball next to me as the rounds pinged off the Hummer. I shifted to my side and pulled my legs up to my chest to prevent a ricochet from finding one of them.

"Otto, since we might die today, I have to know something. Why are all the Hammer brothers named after actual hammers? It's odd, right?"

I craned my neck to face him. I wanted him to see the shock on my face but only caused my neck to cramp. Now I was shocked AND injured. "Randy, that may be the saddest thing I've ever heard. You think we may die, and the most pressing thought you have, the solitary question you need answered, is my parents' naming convention. Not, *hey, do you think we'll go to heaven* or *what's the meaning of life?* Not even *why are dead people trying to eat us?* So sad."

"Naming convention? Word of the day calendar, Otto?"

I started to reply, but Randy cut in. "No, it's not my only question. My other question is also about the Hammer clan. So spill it. I can't die not knowing the answer."

Stone raised his fist, but we didn't fire. The rounds flying from the window kept us from raising weapons. I was running short on patience and the BSU soldiers needed to pay the price. I shook my head at Stone, patted my ear, and pointed up. Not your standard-issue hand signal, but it got the message across. Stone understood, and his three quick shots were drowned out by the BSU soldier's onslaught.

"Okay, listen up. My dad worked construction, and his first job was running a jackhammer. That gave us Jackson. Jackhammers are used on stone; that's an easy one. Otto is a variation of the automatic-hammer. He was German, so thank God he went with Otto and not Auto. Does that do it for you? Will you die with a smile on your face?"

A string of shots tore up the sod where my legs had been, ending our bizarre conversation.

Randy said it first. "They changed firing angles. We can't hold this position much longer."

He was right. We needed to break the stalemate.

"Okay, let's figure something out."

"What, no strategy or tactics talk? Just plain ol' figure something out?"

While I geared up for an appropriately abrasive response, a round exploded through the Hummer's fender, sending shrapnel deep into my cheek. I brought my left hand to the wound and pulled it back to find it dripping with blood. My blood!

I didn't realize I had broken from cover until Randy and Lisa started screaming at me to stop. Rounds pelted the ground to my left, but rage blinded me and I continued my charge.

"You shot me, you son-of-a-bitch! I'm coming for your ass!" I screamed.

My face a bloody, anger-twisted mess, I launched my body at the door. Bone-crushing pain consumed me an instant later.

CHAPTER 5
COUNTERMEASURES

Packet stared out the conference room window on the fifth floor of the capital building. The chaos in the streets below enraged him. "You are responsible for this, Choke. You have destroyed our home."

Choke's hands covered his bowed face, his world spinning from his collision with the heavy wooden column and the realization that his beloved DPRK was being annihilated. Screams of the dying competing with gunfire battered his ears. He needn't witness the carnage; he knew the destructive power of his mutated weapon.

But he would not shoulder the blame for the death of his land. "I'll remind you, Packet, you unleashed the weapon on our soil."

Packet pivoted and stormed to Choke's side, slapping his hands from his face. "No, Choke. This rests on your soul and yours only! You should have forced your scientists to conduct comprehensive testing. We would have known the results when injected into a junkie. Instead, you insisted the weapon was ready. Dear Leader should have killed me and then died before spreading the virus. He is now but a monster, hogtied and craving human flesh."

Packet paused as their phones buzzed. A quick glance at his, then Dear Leader's confirmed his assumption. The military was seeking guidance.

Packet didn't bother with customary military salutations. "General Ri, kill them all. Order your army to slaughter anyone outside their home."

The line was silent except for the sounds of battle raging in the background. "General Ri, should I demonstrate my direction on you so your men know how to proceed?"

A full twenty seconds passed before Ri replied, "Vice Chair Packet, is that Dear Leader's direction? I cannot reach him, but I trust he would not want his people murdered."

Blinded by rage at Ri's insubordination, Packet spat his reply, "Dear Leader no longer controls the DPRK. He has retreated to Mount Paektu. I'm in command, and I order you to destroy anyone walking the streets. A virus has infected our land. A virus from the West is causing our people to crave human flesh. We must contain it."

"Honorable Packet, our army will crush the virus like a spider under our boots."

Packet's reptilian smile dominated his features. The mention of the West had its desired effect. Ri would now follow any direction blindly; he would focus solely on destroying the plague. His hatred of the West would override any critical thinking; nothing would stand in Ri's path to victory.

"Your actions are honorable, Ri. Intelligence has reported that China, Russia, our brothers to our South, and America have plotted against us. We are at war with the world. Listen closely to my orders." He paused as his plan festered to life. Packet was determined to live and to destroy the imperialists. But first, he needed to escape the madness befalling his home.

Referencing the "Map of the Ultimate War Plan," renamed Operation Ultimate, which had hung in the conference room since the war with the imperialists, he rattled off his orders: "Deploy the entirety of our infantry into the streets. They are to eliminate everyone they encounter. We are proceeding with Operation Ultimate."

Packet's declaration forced a gasp from Ri, who quickly recovered his composure as Packet continued. "Launch missiles from Yongjo-ri and Sohae into China. Launch missiles from Sangnam-ri into Russia. Launch missiles from Musudan-ri into Japan."

Packet paused, once again consulting the Map and allowing General Ri time to scribble the orders on his notepad.

"Deploy the 1st Air Combat Division to China. Deploy the 8th Air Combat Division to the USSR. Begin bombardment of the South." Packet's eyes searched the map for his escape and landed on Namp'o Naval Command. "Order the 820th Armored Corps to send an armored personnel carrier to the capital. They will provide transport for First Vice Chair Choke and me. They will take us to Namp'o.

Order the remaining assets from the 820th to rendezvous with us for embarkation from Namp'o. Direct ALL naval assets to launch and rendezvous at Longitude 131E, Latitude 38N. We are invading America!"

Ri sat, stunned, his dream finally seeing the light of day. He would witness the fall of the great American imperialist nation. His reverie was quickly broken by reality. "Vice Chair Packet, your orders bring me great joy. But Sir, many ships in our fleet lack the range to reach America. Should we redirect them to attack the South to divert attention away from our movement?"

Packet nearly broke into laughter at the ease with which he had manipulated Ri. His bloodlust had become Packet's toy to play with. "General Ri, that is a most superior tactic. Make it happen. The 9th and 10th Mechanized Corps will embark with our armada. All others will execute Operation Ultimate. They will fight, to the last man, for the DPRK. Move now, Ri. The virus is spreading."

Packet disconnected the call and returned Choke's glare. Recognizing the question in the man's eyes, he answered the unspoken words. "No, our families will not join us. They will sacrifice their lives for the mighty DPRK." Choke's sobbing reaction to the devastating news brought yet another round of demonic laughter from Packet as the sounds of destruction reached a fevered pitch outside the conference room window.

CHAPTER 6
AEROSOLIZED

"Doctor McCune, I need a progress report."

McCune noticed the man's voice was stretched thin with urgency. He exhibited none of his usual optimism or pleasantries.

The pressure of McCune's work had already pounded his soul to dust. He didn't need a government official standing on his neck while he worked—especially one possessing scant understanding of the complexity of virology. *Please go back to licking the boots of the politicians you serve and allow me to work.* A faint smile creased his exhausted features at his musings.

He chose his words carefully. "We have only observed the formula in two virus mutations. The antidote defeated both." He paused to review the research paper then continued, "We were unable to gather any data after defeating the virus. The damage they sustained while infected was too great and killed them."

"Which mutation levels were tested?"

McCune's tone reflected his annoyance with the interruption. "We have conducted tests at level zero, which possess no advanced skills. And level one mutation, where the subject exhibits rudimentary vocalization skills. I'm referring to that terrible rasping. We need to test a level two subject. Level two mutations exhibit basic reasoning skills. Akin to a child avoiding fire the second time he encounters it because it burned him the first time. They also possess level one mutation abilities."

McCune paused to review his notes, then continued, "Work on a delivery system begins in phase two. With no heartbeat, we're struggling to determine the most efficient method for administering the antidote."

"Can it be aerosolized?"

The question stunned McCune. "Is that an actual question, or merely a vocalized thought? We possess incomplete data—."

The voice sliced through his statement. "Doctor, you've noticed their progression, correct?" The voice continued before McCune could answer. "They are advancing at an alarming rate, Doctor. How long until complex reasoning abilities appear? They recently developed pack-hunting strategies. What's next—using weapons? I needn't remind you that the primal instinct of any organism is survival. Meaning, the organism evolves to sate that instinct. Now, answer my question."

McCune, taken aback by the brisk lecture, refused to change his stance. "We must test it on level two mutations. Furthermore, if it is aerosolized we must conduct human trials. A treatment will do us no good if it eliminates the surviving population. I'll stress again, this is a cure, not a vaccine. Find me several level two mutations and willing, uninfected, humans. Remember, level two mutations demonstrate basic dexterity. So keep your doors locked."

McCune slammed his encrypted phone to the polished metal lab table, resulting in a resounding gong that startled his team to stiffness. "My apologies. I possess little patience for the tyrants this virus has created."

He searched the faces of his small team. Vacant eyes, circled with skin so dark they appeared to have been beaten, stared back at him with fearful anticipation. They had been pushed, relentlessly, to develop a response to the virus. Their failures outnumbered progress by immeasurable numbers, until now. They stood on the cusp of saving the world.

The silence permeating the makeshift lab became unbearable as his team awaited direction. His uncharacteristic outburst signaled that yet another directional change loomed.

"Begin testing the antidote's sustainability when Ciprofloxacin and Levofloxacin function as a host."

"Doctor McCune, is the antidote to be aerosolized? An enormous amount of testing needs to be completed before we can determine an effective delivery method. They don't breathe. How will the antidote enter their system?"

Jill Kris was arguably the most knowledgeable individual on McCune's team. Her background in virology was unparalleled. Her concern was anchored in science, and the complexity of this new direction was immense. They needed to remain focused, and he needed Jill's unquestioning support.

"Doctor Kris, yes, that is our new direction. I understand the implications. However, our government does not." McCune breathed deep before continuing, "We possess the knowledge, in this lab, to eliminate the virus. Our breakthrough was extraordinary. We must now dig deeper within ourselves to deliver our world from extinction! I beg you to rise above the limitations of your knowledge and bend the science to do our bidding."

Chapter 7
Eight of Nine

Debris exploded from the wall, pelting Shafter as he awaited his execution. His mind whirled, attempting to reconcile what it witnessed.

The dust hadn't settled before a second explosion sent him airborne. An instant before the room's steel entry door pinned him to the wall, crushing the wind from his lungs, he realized the hotel was under attack.

The instinct to flee was overwhelming, but Shafter resisted. Instead, he slithered under the protective girth of the door that had saved his life by shielding him from the destructive force unleashed by the blast.

His world filled with the sounds of war as explosions pummeled the wooden frame of the once beautiful hotel. The unseen assailants found their mark and delivered him to Hell's gate.

From beneath the door, he spied his unconscious executioner sprawled out and covered in wreckage. Shafter dared to reach out and secure the handgun now abandoned on the floor. The gun felt foreign in his hand. He stared at it with the wide-eyed wonderment of a child on Santa's lap and read aloud, "M9 Berretta."

In that instant, his power-obsessed brain chose to live and began forming a plan.

"That's only eight of my nine lives. Try harder next time!" he screamed over the din of battle.

The building shook violently as rubble rained down around him. With each salvo, his body instinctively pulled into a tighter ball, seeking protection under the door. He buried his face in bent arms, attempting to shield both his head and hearing from the destruction.

"How much ammunition did you bring? We would have surrendered had you asked," he barked as the fear of dying permeated his thoughts for the second time in under an hour. Tears streaked his dirt-covered face. "I deserve better than to die like this."

"They don't care," a voice yelled. "They want you dead, and dead you will be if this keeps up."

Shafter yelped in fear at the voice seemingly delivered from heaven. He pulled his head from his arms and searched for the voice's source through the haze. A hand grabbed his lapel, yanking him forward.

"Where's my gun?"

Shafter was face to bleeding face with his executioner, "You mean this?" he asked as he pointed the handgun at his assassin.

The man laughed, despite their situation, as Shafter's hand trembled. "Take your finger off the trigger, you ass."

"Shut UP! I hold the gun, which makes YOU the ass."

The man released Shafter and, in one smooth motion, redirected the gun, bent his wrist up, and disarmed him. "Never point a gun at something you aren't willing to destroy," he said, then pistol-whipped Shafter, knocking him unconscious.

Chapter 8
Rapid Response

Tanks rumbled down the street, supporting a line of infantrymen shooting anyone, living or undead, caught in the open. Children, women, the old, and the young were indiscriminately massacred, their blood staining the street a deep red.

The sounds overwhelmed Choke as he perched in a window overlooking Mansudane Street as his beloved country, his home, devoured itself.

He watched an undead flank a line of foot soldiers and sink filthy teeth deep into the neck of a man no older than twenty years old, his screams piercing the thunder of battle while blood arched several feet into the air from his severed carotid artery.

Horror raced through Choke as the soldier's comrades rushed to his aid. He understood that their valiant efforts had condemned them to death. He tried to force a warning from his throat, to order them to abandon the wounded man, but he sat paralyzed by remorse and only shook his head as the soldier's arterial spray drenched his friends with his blood. *The world is ending.*

A loud thud followed by a sound similar to a bowling ball rolling along a highly polished alley broke his trance.

"What will we do with Dear Leader?" Choke asked. "If Ri or any of the others find him, they will execute us." Receiving demented laughter in response, he quickly glanced in Packet's direction. The power-crazed man stood in the doorway to Dear Leader's private quarters, holding his blood-soaked hands up for Choke's viewing pleasure.

"Please, Mister Choke. Do you still view yourself as having a superior intellect? Look at your feet. I have already addressed the issue. No one will find him!"

Choke gasped as Packet's meaning became clear. Dear Leader's severed head rested at his feet, its jagged flaps of skin highlighting the crudeness with which Packet had removed it from its body. Packet had forced a letter opener deep into Dear Leader's eye socket then used his bare hands to perform the repulsive deed.

Choke retched and moved to escape the accusatory glare of Dear Leader when the sounds of boots slapping the marble floor outside the conference room spurred him to action. His fear of dying overriding his repulsion from the severed head, he snatched it from the floor and heaved it out the window. Turning back to Packet, he shouted as he ran in his direction, "Grab his arms, we must hide him before they enter."

As the men fought to stuff the putrefying body of their former ruler under his bed, a ground-shaking explosion plunged them into darkness. Dozens more followed in quick succession, trailed by the roar of powerful jet engines.

Packet screamed over the reverberation of the high explosives leveling the capital city, "This can't be our military. They were not ordered to bomb the city. We are under attack."

Another blast sent shards of glass hurling through the air as plaster rained down on the men struggling to conceal Dear Leader's girth from sight.

Choke barked, "No time. We must leave NOW."

Dropping the corpse to the marble floor, the men reached the door as Ri's men kicked it from its hinges. Weapon-mounted lights pierced the darkened room, landing on the dust-covered faces of Choke and Packet.

"Speak, or we will kill you!" a frantic soldier shouted while lining them up in the sights of his Type 88 rifle.

Packet screamed, "We're not infected, we are both alive. Get us to safety, no matter the cost!"

The soldier understood the order; he had to save these men, even if it meant sacrificing his life. He'd be proud to do so!

"Fall in between us. We'll escort—."

Another blast cut the soldier off and propelled enormous chunks of debris through the room, forcing the men to take cover under the oversized conference table. When the dust settled, they found the soldier dead, a jagged hunk of timber jutting from his chest. Sunlight spilled from a ragged hole where a wall once stood, giving them an unobstructed view of the Chinese Xian H6 bombers flying unopposed above their capital. China had mounted a rapid response to Packet's diversionary tactic.

A second soldier assumed command, ordering the men to follow the squad. Bedlam greeted them on the streets of the capital, overwhelming their senses. Mangled bodies lay strewn about the steps leading to the idling Chunma-D armored personnel carrier. The APC's turret gun sent a stream of 7.62mm rounds into hordes of living and undead converging on the area.

Packet climbed the rails to the entry hatch but stopped when the turret gunner ceased fire as a group of school children filled the sights of the heavy machinegun. He shouted at the gunner while slithering into the safety of the APC, "Kill them all! We cannot determine if they're infected. We must sacrifice them for the survival of our glorious DPRK."

Packet received the response he desired as the soldier leveled the turret gun on the children and sprayed hundreds of rounds into their tiny bodies.

Black smoke belched from the enormous machine as the driver slammed the accelerator to the floor. Packet's seat afforded him an unobstructed view through the small bulletproof-glass windshield. Frantic people flooded their path; it seemed the entire populace now blocked their escape.

Packet barked, "Drive this beast to Namp'o and directly onto the first ship you see. Don't stop for any reason."

The APC plowed through the masses as it departed the capital building. The desperate living slammed against the thick metal armor, creating a drumbeat of hopelessness as they realized the military wasn't there to rescue them.

Choke watched the madness through a side-mounted viewing port. Tormented faces flashed across the glass while the APC rumbled to safety. After they broke free of the mob, he noticed a group chasing them and gasped in horror as his creations pulled them to the pavement and ripped them apart. He landed hard in a troop seat and let his tears flow freely. The realization gripped him … *I have ended the world!*

CHAPTER 9
STRIPE

Man, the sky looks beautiful today. But why can I see it from inside the house? Why does my shoulder, neck, and head hurt so badly? My view and thoughts were interrupted when Stone's legs filled my vision, his Tavor rapidly barking 62 Grain Green Tips into the metal door's handle. I turned my head to shield my face from the resulting shrapnel and found Lisa crouched at my side.

A moment later, hell broke loose around me. The distinct sound of Randy's .308 blazing to life joined Stone's Tavor and Lisa yelling for me to stand. Got it. I'm still outside and on the ground.

"So, I didn't breach the door?" I asked.

"No. But you almost got yourself killed. Get up and join the fight that you started."

Still a little hazy, I asked, "Did you almost shoot me again, Lisa?"

She brought her Sig Carbine over her shoulder and pointed the stock at my face.

Flinching, I yelled, "Don't you do it, Lisa. I'm already wounded."

"Otto! SHUT UP and follow Stone. Randy can't cover us forever."

I lifted my head and peered down the length of my body and through the open door. Stone had taken a covering position and waited for us to move into position.

I shot to my feet and immediately regretted it as a wave of nausea swept over me. Fighting the urge to throw up, I entered the house, followed by Lisa, and headed for the stairs, where I took cover against the wall that opened to the staircase.

The house was filthy. A small trash-heaped table, surrounded by folding chairs, sat in the center of the main room. A kitchenette flanked our position on the opposite side of the first floor. Blacked-out patio doors filled the space along its back wall. Debris littered the floor, and the walls were smeared with grime; the sickly stench of rotting food saturated the compact, windowless living space.

Randy continued to send round after round into the second-story window. His assault quieted our targets' guns, but they still held the advantage.

I yelled to our enemy, "You've lost! Throw us your weapons and you might live." I really didn't know if they would. RAM's new policy on combatants was a hard line. No prisoners. However, if they had information, they might squeak past dying and live a miserable life in confinement. I didn't care which; I only wanted to go home. Well, throw up and then go home.

"Listen, I don't feel good, Lisa is mad as a hornet, Stone can shoot your eyes out before you blink, and the best shot in Northeast Ohio has your only exit covered. What say you? Maybe give us a break and surrender?"

I glanced at Lisa and found her bug-eyes glaring at me, "What?" I asked.

"Why am I *angry*, but Randy and Stone are *super soldiers*?"

"Because it's, oh I don't know, TRUE."

Leaning close to me, Lisa said, "Remember, I'm behind you. Hopefully, I don't get a twitchy trigger finger when we head upstairs."

Lisa scares me.

After a long, hard look into Lisa's unblinking eyes, I decided to move things along. My head was pounding, my nausea was giving me the sweats, and Lisa had just threatened to kill me for the umpteenth time. I needed to get home.

"Okay, obviously you found the information I shared with you uninspiring. That's a real shame. I thought we could be friends, but have it your way." I grabbed a handful of garbage from the floor and tossed it into the stairwell where it was shot into even smaller pieces of garbage.

Turning away from the dust and fragments flying in every direction, I came nose to nose with Lisa.

"If you try to kiss me, I will knock your front teeth out," she grumbled.

"As tempting as your offer is, I'd rather have one of your flash-bangs."

"Excellent choice, Otto," Stone chirped from his position.

"Thanks, brother. I'm glad someone appreciates me."

Rolling her eyes, Lisa shoved the flash-bang into my hand. I turned, pulled the pin, and tossed it up the stairs as hundreds of rounds again exited from the stairwell.

The explosion from the device easily penetrated my hands as they covered my ears.

We waited a ten-count then made our move towards the stairs when a beautiful sound, similar to the zipper on my prom date's pink chiffon dress being undone, reached us. Randy had brought the M249 online and was pummeling the second story.

I put a fist up and halted our advance, waiting for the M249 to cease her devastating assault. The sound of wood splintering was joined by a voice screaming something unintelligible.

The M249 fell silent, and I gave the signal to advance. Five steps from the second-floor landing, I signaled a halt. The stairs dumped into a wide hallway with one room on either side. On my left sat the room they had occupied while pinning us down in the street. Its door hung ajar, affording me an unobstructed view to most of its interior. It was a shattered mess of bullet-riddled drywall, broken glass, destroyed office furniture, and the dust from Randy's barrage still hanging in the air. I detected no movement, saw no dead bodies, and found no sign of our enemy. The door to the other room was closed.

My heart was pounding in my ears, and sweat poured down my body. Here I was again, getting ready to charge into the unknown and possibly get myself, or others, killed. Another wave of nausea hit me. I was sure I had a concussion.

I whispered to Lisa, "How many flash-bangs are left?"

"Two."

"Okay, give me one and follow me when I give the signal. I have a plan."

Lisa handed me one of her flash-bangs and stared at me expectantly while I placed it on the stair in front of me.

"It's in my head, Lisa, and I think I've been concussed and won't be able to explain it to you. Just follow me when I move."

"What the hell does that mean, Otto?"

"You know, I have a concussion. I was concussed when I hit the door."

"Huh, if that's true, I don't want to follow you anywhere. That includes into a hallway with people shooting at me."

"Relax, I got this," I said, rolling my eyes dismissively.

I picked up a six-inch-long hunk of drywall and tossed it into the hallway before Lisa could voice another objection. When it slapped against the hardwood floor, bullets exploded through the walls of both rooms. I fired into the room with the closed door until my bolt locked back.

I swapped magazines, released the bolt catch, grabbed the flash-bang, and tossed it into the room with the open door. As I watched it sail through the air, I realized the pin remained firmly in place.

"Lisa, I need your second flash-bang."

"Are you kidding me?" Lisa howled while fumbling to retrieve the device.

"Oh my God, hand it over before that idiot figures out I gave him a perfectly good flash-bang."

I turned towards the room and caught the BSU soldier making his move.

This time, I pulled the pin *then* tossed the device into the room, covered my ears, and ducked.

A thunderous boom smacked my brain when the flash-bang detonated. I shook off the shock, and we moved into the hall. Stone broke right, sending half a dozen rounds through the closed door before kicking it open and rushing into the room.

Lisa stacked up behind me as I *sliced the pie* from the hallway into the room. At about halfway through my slice, I spotted him. A thrashing form lay on his side, clothes smoldering and hands covering his ears. It looked like he'd stood on top of my flash-bang when it detonated, knocking him out of the fight.

I rushed forward then to my left and engaged the BSU soldier as Lisa entered and broke right, clearing every crevasse of the tiny room.

She gave the all-clear the same instant Stone entered the room.

"One dead in the other room, a small amount of ammo, and loads of food supplies."

As I stood over the soldier, he became aware of our presence. His eyes went buggy, and he reached for the M16 lying next to him. I stepped on his hand, shifting all of my weight on it while placing my AR's muzzle on his cheek. "That's a terrible idea, friend."

Lisa moved in and kicked the weapon to the corner, then grabbed two zip cuffs from her dump pouch and secured his hands.

I noticed the soldier's stature and was stunned. "He's just a kid, for God's sake. How old are you, fourteen?"

He didn't respond as he struggled to free his hands. I increased the pressure of my gun on his cheek and asked again.

He glared at me from the corner of his eye and screamed, "I see your lips moving, but I can't hear you, dumbass. You know, from the flash-bang."

He had a point, but I didn't like his attitude and felt I should remind him he'd shot first. So I poked him in his glaring eye with the barrel of my gun. "Now you're deaf AND blind, DUMBASS!" I whipped my head around. "Lisa, Stone, get this ass-face to his feet."

I kept my weapon trained on him while Lisa grabbed his hair and pulled him to a sitting position, allowing Stone to grab him under his armpits and yank him to his feet.

The sight which greeted me was confusing. His face said he was in his twenties; his body said he was eleven years old. It was creepy.

As soon as he got to his feet, he made a move for the door; Lisa rewarded him with a brutal right-cross. The sound of bone crunching accompanied by blood flowing over his chin confirmed she had, indeed, broken Shorty's nose.

"Now you're deaf, blind, and can't smell. Keep it up and I'll cut your fingers off and remove your tongue. Then you'll have no senses left." I paused, letting my joke sink in. It didn't. "Get it, you'll make no sense."

I was pleased with my wittiness under pressure but found Lisa and Stone weren't. They stared at me for a long minute before our combatant made another move. Head leading the way, he let loose a battle cry and charged me. He caught me off guard but not Stone as he tapped the side of his head with his rifle's stock, sending him crashing to the ground.

"Pay attention, Otto. The little shit almost took you out."

"No, Stone. He didn't *almost take me out*. It was part of my plan, you just interrupted—."

Stone cut me off. "Ooooh, got it. You're a talented actor then. Because I saw my brother caught flat-footed and almost killed."

"Killed is a little dramatic, don't you think? And I am an excellent actor. I have you fooled that I like you. So there's that."

The BSU soldier recovered from the blow and launched a litany of insults at us. He frothed at the mouth as he offended the size of our man parts, where we lived, and our guns ... our guns! He avoided insulting Lisa, more than likely to avoid another vicious right-cross.

"Yo, Stripe. Did you eat after midnight?" I asked the frenzied soldier. "You know what? Every time I look at you, a song by Gary Newman pops into my head." Lisa and Stone burst out laughing at the inference.

Our levity sent the soldier into a fresh rage. But our attention was yanked away when a yelp followed by gunfire roared through the windows. We'd forgotten about Randy!

CHAPTER 10
FLOATING TO THE TOP

Shafter woke. He found himself staring into the face of his executioner, now huddled with him under the protection of the steel door.

In a low, harsh whisper, the soldier said, "Keep your mouth shut, Shafter."

As the haze cleared from his eyes, Shafter found the command insulting—downright insubordinate—and fury overtook his emotions. "What's your name?" he asked.

"I told you to shut up. You may not care if you die, but I do."

Shafter reached up and found blood tricking from his gashed forehead. Rubbing the blood between his fingers, he couldn't keep his pompous mouth shut. "Seems you already tried to kill me and failed, twice. Now answer my question."

The soldier maneuvered his hand between them, covering Shafter's mouth in a tight grip. "Do you hear that?" he asked while motioning skyward with his eyes. "That's the sound of death searching for your pathetic hide."

Shafter stopped struggling against the soldier's powerful grip and noticed the thumping of helicopter blades in the distance. The rattle of full-auto gunfire caused him to flinch.

"If you blow our cover, I'll use your mushy body as a shield. Clear?"

Shafter nodded his compliance and the executioner released his grip then fixed him with a hard stare, promising pain if he failed to remain silent.

As the warbird strafed the building and its grounds, Shafter noticed the sounds of human suffering mixed in with the clatter of hellfire. He realized their assailants were mopping up instead of taking prisoners. RAM had shifted its policy. No mercy would be shown, no lives spared, and no shelter from the storm offered.

Shafter's corrupted mind raced, searching for a way out of this fresh Hell. The tumblers began clicking into place when another explosion rocked the building. The sensation of weightlessness forced a startled scream from his throat. He screwed his eyes shut, expecting the impact of the soldier's blow, or worse, a bullet to the brain. Instead, his body slammed to the ground. Something heavy fell on him, forcing the air from his lungs. It was the door, he realized hazily.

Smoke-filtered sunshine forced him to squint. His surroundings were confusing. Jagged wood, scorched black, smoldered around him. Mangled furniture was piled atop the wreckage of battle, reminiscent of Europe during Hitler's siege.

His executioner had disappeared, but the helicopter had not. It hovered over his safe space, whirling debris into his face as it waited for him to show himself. *They can't know I'm here*, he thought. *They're waiting for any survivors to make a fatal mistake.* "Not today, RAM scum. Today, I win!" he yelled over the war machine's thumping blades.

A voice admonished his bravado-laced declaration, "That's the most ridiculous thing I've ever heard. But you are a politician, so I'm not surprised."

Shafter squirmed as he tried to find the source of the insult. His executioner lay motionless under a pile of drywall a few feet away. The dust-covered man blended into his surroundings like a chameleon.

"If you call this winning, I now understand why the election surprised you."

Shafter bristled at the comment. "They stole that election. None of this would have happened if we had won. I'd be in Washington—."

"Shafter, shut up!" his assassin screamed. "You can explain how you know this wouldn't have happened later. Now, shut your mouth."

The copter moved quickly to an unseen position and brought its guns to life, raining death onto unseen victims.

"Remain perfectly still and silent until I tell you to move."

"Excuse me, Mister Executioner-man. You answer to *me*. I'll determine when I can move."

The dusty killer moved his right hand enough to point his gun at Shafter.

Stuttering at the unspoken threat, he said, "I planned on remaining undercover until our mutual enemy retreats. Your threat is unwarranted."

"Shut that pompous mouth, or I'll gleefully kill you."

Shafter sulked under the door for twenty agonizing minutes as RAM's military repeatedly ignored their section of the destroyed hotel. The pause allowed him to plot his escape. But escape to where? BSU no longer existed, and RAM had made its intentions clear. He was a ruler with no peasants to lord over. Surely, some fragments of BSU government had survived. President Wharton had been in hiding just a few short weeks ago. If he could contact her, he would easily squirm his way back into power.

"Piles' phone!" he murmured. "I must find Piles' phone."

Shocked from his reverie by a hand gripping his mouth, Shafter flailed in full-blown panic. The grip tightened the more he fought against it.

Finally, the owner of the hand whispered, "Stop struggling and keep your mouth shut. The attack has stopped. But RAM may have boots on the ground, so zip it."

Ten minutes later, Shafter struggled to push the door off his body, prompting a sarcastic laugh from the man who was now pivotal to his survival. "Help me, soldier boy, or I'll leave you behind. And what the Hell is your name?"

"Banks, the name is Banks. Shafter, rethink your threat. You can't even lift thirty pounds. How long do you think you'll live without me?"

The statement signaled to Shafter that Banks understood the dynamic of their relationship. Each had a vital role to play in their survival.

Banks lifted the door, freeing Shafter. He stood and brushed at his suit. He quickly realized he was standing on the ground floor of the war-torn hotel. Confusion clouded his features as he spun around, taking in the surreal landscape.

Banks said, "They destroyed the load-bearing walls, sending us straight down. The only reason the roof didn't crush us is because of the wreckage piled up around our position. A foot in either direction and we'd be dead."

Shafter regarded the man with a cynical stare but held his tongue.

"What's the plan?"

"Well, Mister Banks, we find Piles, or what's left of her, and relieve her of her phone."

Bewildered, Banks said, "Really? That's the plan. Make some calls and get reinforcements sent? Oh, I know, have them send a car for us. I prefer a limo."

Shafter's urge to belittle Banks was all-consuming. But he realized he needed the man and softened his approach. "Oh, ye of little faith. Trust me when I tell you I'm very well connected. You do your part, and I'll do mine, and we will live to reap our revenge on RAM."

Banks held zero confidence in Shafter's ability to deliver them to safety. But his only other option was to go it alone in a foreign country with few resources.

"Shafter, if I get bitten, I will eat your worthless carcass first. Lead the way, Mister Connected Politician."

Shafter moved from the wreckage and tried to orient himself. The hotel was destroyed, leaving few discernible landmarks intact. The twisted bodies of BSU soldiers and slaughtered zombies littered the hotel grounds. Thick smoke wafted from smoldering wreckage, further confusing Shafter's attempt to get his directional bearings.

Focusing on the hotel's street-level marquee helped him locate what used to be the main entrance to the building. The conference room where he had last seen Piles was located behind the lobby.

He started walking towards the ruined lobby and quickly found himself forced to climb over heaps of destroyed furniture and drywall. His Cole Haans offered no traction as he slipped and fell knees first onto a shattered window. He howled in agony as the glass pierced his skin.

"Shafter, shut up. You're ringing the dinner bell for every zombie within ten miles."

Shafter went to his hands, trying to shift the pressure from knees only to slam them into more jagged glass. Biting back the pain, he struggled to stand and survey his damaged body. Blood soaked his suit pants and dripped from dozens of cuts on his hands. A whimper escaped his mouth as he picked a sizeable chunk of glass from the palm of his right hand.

"You'll want to cover those wounds. If they get infected, you'll probably die."

Shafter looked around, attempting to find Banks. He located the soldier sitting on a tattered chair in the destroyed lobby. His wide grin told Shafter that Banks was enjoying his pain.

"What the hell are you doing? How did you get past me?" Shafter demanded.

"In the future, you will communicate your intentions, Mister Senator. More importantly, you will follow my direction. Have I been clear?"

Shafter managed a nod and asked, "How do I get to you without killing myself?"

After he finished laughing, Banks pointed out the path Shafter had missed when he started his journey to the lobby.

After twenty minutes of searching, they found the body of Senator Cortina under a conference room table, but no sign of Finkelstein or Piles. At a loss on how to continue, Shafter kicked a pile of rubble in frustration and turned to Banks to voice his displeasure when a screeched plea for help reached them. Stock-still, both men waited for the terrible noise to repeat. Again the plea came, and Banks locked onto the location and bolted in its direction.

They began rummaging through wreckage in the area when movement from under an enormous support beam caught Shafter's eye. He rushed to the spot, ignoring the pain from his hands while furiously searching through the ruins.

Banks joined him and together they lifted a large section of drywall resting atop the rubble. A mascara-streaked face glared at them from under the beam. They had found Piles, and the hagfish was still alive.

"Shafter, stop staring at me like an idiot and get me out of here, you stupid bastard."

"Hello, Madam Senator, you look … shall I say, like death warmed over."

"Shafter, you being alive is proof that shit always floats to the top."

Shafter removed more debris from Piles' withered body only to discover she was trapped under a massive support beam. Her legs were twisted at unhealthy angles and soaked in blood. He needed the phone; he needed her to tell him where it was.

"Piles, while I work to get this off of you, tell Banks where your bag is so we don't lose all of our notes."

"Do I look like an idiot, Shafter? Nothing happens until I'm freed."

Piles shifted her head, trying to locate her phone and her bag. There it lay. Shafter's ticket out of this nightmare; her phone had been hidden under her head.

Meanwhile, Banks had been searching the area for the phone. He held up Piles' bag and showed it to Shafter.

A slimy smile broke over Shafter's face, but the rasping of the dead interrupted his joy.

"We need to go!" Banks yelled.

"You will not leave me here, Shafter."

Shafter looked toward the approaching dead. "Can you speak a little louder, please? I couldn't hear you."

His question had the desired effect, sending Piles into a rage. Her verbal abuse rose to a crescendo after Shafter said, "Oh, let me help you with that," then brushed dirt into her eyes. "It's better you don't see what's coming for you." Then he grabbed a jagged hunk of wood and slammed it into Piles' shoulder. "Just a little assurance that you keep screeching. I wouldn't want your dinner guests to miss the main course."

With that, he grabbed her phone and ran to Banks' position. "We have what we need. Time for you to do your part."

Banks glared at Shafter then picked up a piece of twisted rebar, shoving it into Shafter's quivering hand.

"You'll want to swing that behind you as hard as your soft little body can."

Shafter's eyes went wide when he realized what Banks meant. He pivoted without hesitation, holding the rebar in his outstretched hand. The wet crunch of metal crushing rotted skull shocked him. The monster fell motionless as Shafter's chest heaved from exertion. He glanced up to find dozens of zombies on the march. Panic overtaking him, he turned back to find Banks running for his life.

After a moment of hesitation, Shafter followed Banks' lead. More monsters converged on the area as the thought of fighting for his life forced tears down his face.

Banks heard Shafter weeping and yelled, "Stop blubbering and run, you idiot."

Shafter's heart pounded in his ears and he struggled to keep Banks in sight. His thoughts turned to quitting when suddenly a piercing scream reached him. He glanced over his shoulder just as a zombie collapsed onto Piles. Blood arced as the beast wrenched skin from her throat. Dozens more joined the feast until the writhing mound resembled a vulture's feeding frenzy.

Shafter turned his attention back to pursuing Banks, but the man had disappeared. He howled with a mixture of anger and despair when a hard tug on his tattered suit jacket slammed him to the ground.

He screamed and swung the rebar wildly, trying to fend off his attacker. His arms were pinned forcefully to his chest at the same time Banks came into focus.

"STOP!" Banks commanded. "You'll draw them right to us. If that happens, I'll slit your throat and feed your worthless skin to them."

Shafter struggled to gain control of his emotions, but Banks dragged him to where he had holed up, forcing another shocked yelp. Banks shook him, again ordering him to shut up while pulling him to his feet.

"We're near the carport. We should be able to find a hiding place and work on a plan."

"Do you think we'll find a car that runs?" Shafter asked hopefully.

"Doubtful, but we don't have a lot of options. The dead have figured out that fresh food is running around, and we need to lie low. Keep your mouth shut and stick to me like glue." Not waiting for confirmation, Banks turned and bolted in the direction of the carport with Shafter on his heels.

As they rounded a partially collapsed wall, Banks threw his fist in the air and knelt low behind some rubble with Shafter following his lead.

In a whisper, Banks asked, "Do you smell that?"

Shafter sniffed around like a bloodhound. "Decay mixed with burning flesh? Why, are you looking to invent a new candle scent?"

"No asshole, exhaust. I smell engine exhaust. We need to find the vehicle it's coming from."

Banks was on the move a second later and zeroed in on an area obscured by a partially collapsed metal roof. As he grew closer, he detected the sound of an idling engine.

"Hot damn. One of my boys lived. Let's go."

"If he's alive, why didn't he leave?"

The question slowed Banks' approach. Shafter was right; whoever was in the vehicle should have already escaped. He cleared the twisted metal and found a Yukon in perfect condition with a wide-eyed BSU soldier at the wheel.

The boyish soldier didn't acknowledge Banks as he approached. He just stared out the windshield with his hands on the steering wheel.

Banks walked to the door and pulled it open. The soldier hadn't moved because he was dead. A huge hunk of glass protruded from his abdomen. The coppery scent of blood mixed with the stench of feces overpowered Banks, causing him to gag.

Shafter approached the open door and said, "Well, looks like he zigged when he should have zagged."

The sharp crack to his cheek from Banks' right hand blurred Shafter's vision and nearly knocked him to the ground. "You're lucky I only slapped you. Talk again and I'll rip your lungs out." He turned back to the dead soldier, pried his hands from the steering wheel and lifted him from the seat, then carefully laid him on the ground.

"Get in," he growled.

Banks wiped blood from the instrument panel as Shafter scurried around to the passenger door. The senator had the phone out before Banks put the enormous SUV in gear.

As the Yukon plowed through the wreckage, Shafter found the number he was looking for and hit the sat-phone's call button. He prayed she was still alive as he waited for the call to connect.

His hope soared when the call was answered. "Madam President, this is Senator Shafter. I have important information to share."

CHAPTER 11
FLOTILLA

"Shafter, slow down and repeat the information."

President Wharton rubbed her temples as the senator spoke. The news was stunning. The coalition she'd sanctioned had brought the world to the brink of extinction.

Wharton raged at Shafter, "You power-hungry idiots destroyed everything. At no point did I ask that you annihilate the world. I directed you to reunite America and ensure our BSU government was the ruling party."

The President let Shafter stutter through more information.

"The DPRK has assured me they've developed an antidote. Once it's deployed, we can regain control and force RAM to repel DPRK's invasion. Then we tell the world that BSU cured the virus and retake our place in the power structure."

"Why would the DPRK invade us?"

Shafter took a deep breath before he answered. "The Coalition made *concessions* in exchange for the virus. We agreed to surrender Blue States United territory to the DPRK."

Wharton exploded, "You gave away our country? Is that what I'm hearing? You, in fact, gave our home to a hostile country! I should have you executed. But I won't give you the satisfaction of death. Instead, you will join our flotilla and you WILL fix this."

"Madam President, the blame for the death of BSU rests entirely at the feet of RAM. They forced BSU to attack. RAM caused this."

"I don't disagree with your assessment. However, your actions killed hundreds of millions of people. Actions you took while representing our government. Anything tying BSU to this nightmare must be destroyed. I'll text you our location. Report to me immediately. This conversation is over."

After she texted the coordinates, Wharton hurled the sat-phone across the room, striking her assistant, Amanda, in her stomach and causing her to cry out.

Confusion clouding her features, she asked the President, "Did I do something wrong?"

"No, but consider it an example of what will happen if you cross me." Wharton held Amada in an icy glare before continuing, "Call a staff meeting. I have an urgent matter to discuss."

Amanda stepped to the doorway and said softly, "Jessica, Madam President requests a staff meeting."

Jessica gave an involuntary eye roll at the ridiculous request. *Another staff meeting! You have two staff members, you old windbag. Not the army of staffers you're used to,* Jessica thought from her spot in the main cabin of the yacht.

Before the apocalypse, the seventy-eight-foot, luxuri-ously appointed super-yacht christened *The Flame* would have been a perfect way to spend the summer months. Now, it served as her inescapable super-max prison, an-chored off Hunters Point in San Francisco Bay. Jessica found the endless *staff meetings* exhausting. Wharton was only interested in blaming RAM for BSU's destruction. They never discussed a strategy for beating back the zom-bie hordes. Instead, they grumbled endlessly about blame and revenge. Idiots!

Jessica's thoughts snapped when Wharton bellowed, "Now, Jessica. We need to meet NOW!"

"Yes, Madam President. I'm gathering up my notes."

Wharton launched into her diatribe as Jessica entered the conference room. "Contact our congressional leaders. Direct them to be present in one hour. We may have dis-covered a means to reclaim our country. This meeting is of utmost importance. Attendance is mandatory."

Both women held pens to paper, awaiting further in-struction from Wharton. After a lengthy silence, they glanced up and found Wharton glaring at them. "Move," she barked. "Time is of the essence."

Jessica dreaded her next task. Rounding up the con-gressional leaders for a meeting meant dealing with James O'Brien. The man made her skin crawl. James was a for-mer Protection Club leader; his enormous size was unset-tling, and his penchant for violence was well documented. He used both to his advantage. He enjoyed extorting supplies from other flotilla members, supplies they desperately needed. But that wasn't what she hated; it was his habit of finding a reason to touch her whenever possible. His heavily scarred and calloused hands felt like a cheese-grater when he ran them along any exposed flesh he found.

His role as the group's head of security meant their complaints about his behavior got pushed aside, giving him more power to act as he wanted.

"Hello, my sexy Jessica, to what do I owe the pleasure of hearing your lovely voice?"

Jessica shivered at the sound of James' phlegm-rattled voice seeping through the two-way radio but dutifully carried out the President's orders. "James, you are to summon all congressional leaders to President Wharton's yacht. They will meet her on Deck Three, poolside. They need …"

James spoke over her. "What do I get for my trouble? Maybe you join the meeting in your underwear? That'd be *real* nice."

Jessica gagged, then let her anger answer. "Or, I won't castrate you the next time I see you. Get them to the meeting NOW." She cut off the call.

The women stared at each other in shock before Amanda spoke. "You are my hero! But you better watch yourself; he won't take kindly to the threat."

Jessica knew Amanda was right; James would seek revenge. But the thought of actually castrating him brought a wicked smile to her face. "I know, but I'll have a surprise waiting when he does."

Forty minutes later, the five remaining members of BSU government sat poolside. The blowhards began this meeting as they did each and every meeting. They complained about their living conditions.

"Please, all of you, SHUT UP. I've already told you that where you live is not my concern. If you're unhappy, feel free to scavenge another boat from the monster-filled marina. And before you ask again, you may not move to *The Flame* with me. My security is essential. End of discussion."

She gave each of the members a hard stare to ensure they understood.

After she was comfortable that her proclamation was clear, she continued. "I've recently discovered information that will bring an end to our disgrace. You are here for a conference call. Keep your mouths shut while I negotiate our future."

Wharton produced her sat-phone and a laminated document labeled "World Leaders." Using her index finger, she scanned the document and stopped on the number she sought. She took a deep breath and slowly exhaled as she dialed and hit send.

She activated the speakerphone function and waited as the phone searched for a signal. After a lengthy delay, a heavily accented voice burst from the speaker. The accent drew shocked gasps from every member of the BSU government sitting poolside. Wharton's harsh look silenced them as she spoke, "This is President Wharton of Blue States United calling for Mister Kim."

CHAPTER 12
THANKS, MOM

Dillan stared in disbelief. *This can't be happening. Why did they stop? Did they learn by watching the others fall victim to our defenses? Are they figuring out a way to bypass the barriers to reach the food inside?*

Dillan asked Chuck, "They haven't moved since the leading edge of the herd hit the tripwires? Are you sure?"

Chuck pulled his attention from the troubling scene and gave the same answer he had the first two times Dillan asked. "Not a muscle. They simply stopped and stared at their dead friends." He faced the morbid scene again and said, "Dillan, what's happening? If these things can reason or strategize, we won't be able to build a wall high enough to stop them."

Dillan followed Chuck's gaze back to the landscape beyond the barrier. Dozens of UCs stood motionless, staring at the mangled bodies of the UCs that had fallen victim to the community's defenses.

"Chuck, I don't have an answer for you. But I can say that our barriers performed as intended. I'll ask Will to bring his trainees over for target practice on the remaining UCs. We should take advantage of the opportunity." Dillan remained still, observing the dead. Then he changed his mind. "Let's pike a few first and see what happens."

Chuck gave a nod and called out, "Andrea, pike the leading edge. Everyone else, prepare to fire on my command."

Andrea slid her pike through the fence with a powerful thrust. When the pike pierced her target's skull, the monsters moved as one decayed organism in Andrea's direction. Wet thuds, from bodies slamming onto punji sticks and legs shattering on boulders, quickly rose above the rasps of the dead pursuing their attacker standing behind the fence.

Dozens of molted bodies fell to the community's defenses. None of them stopped their deadly march toward the wall. Dillan noted that they held a singular focus on Andrea's position. They seemed enraged by the death of their comrades.

Ten minutes later, the attack had ended. The stench rising from the battlefield hung thick in the humid summer air. Those UCs not killed during the attack thrashed about, attempting to stand or free themselves from impalement on the punji.

Rapt by the scene, Dillan said, "Pike the ones you can. Let Will's trainees take target practice on the rest." Not receiving a response, he pulled away from the sight and found Chuck staring slack-jawed at the macabre landscape of dead and dying bodies.

"Chuck, you okay?"

Chuck shifted his gaze to Dillan and slowly nodded. "Dillan, what just happened? We were standing in plain sight the whole time, but they didn't move until we killed one of them. Their attack wasn't motivated by hunger. They wanted revenge."

Dillan, unable to counter Chuck's assertion, said, "I'm not sure. But we need to kill the rest and take the bodies to the burn pits."

Mention of the burn pits snapped Chuck from his stupor. "Burn pits! I hate those damn things. I'm not going, Dillan!"

The pits were a recent addition, designed initially to deal with the community's rubbish. Situated two miles from the community, each was over fifteen feet deep and twenty feet long. The stench wafting from them was worse than anything he had ever smelled. It rendered the masks used by the trash collection team useless immediately after they started filling the pits. Even after a burn, the smell brought tears to the eyes of anyone within a mile of them.

Chuck's mishap at the pits last week was the reason for his abrasive response. He'd been helping toss a dead UC into a pit, lost his footing, and tumbled into the slushy mix of burned bodies and festering trash. It took the crew twenty minutes to extract him from the toxic soup. He'd stunk to high heaven for two full days and vowed he'd never go near them again.

Dillan recalled how his mother would manipulate him into doing some of his more unpleasant chores. She'd tell him: *No one is as good at taking out the trash as you. Only you can get the lines straight when you cut the grass.* It was physiological warfare at its finest. And it had prepared him for situations like this.

"Chuck, your team has been talking. They're saying how much they respect you because you're willing to do whatever it takes to make this a better place to live." Dillan took an effectual pause then said, "They'd probably follow you into any situation bec—."

Chuck interrupted Dillan and said, "Dillan, you can stop the BS. I'll take the bodies to the pits. But you owe me, big time." He was silent for a heartbeat, then asked in a hushed voice, "That part about them respecting me. Is it true?" His hopeful expression forced a smile from Dillan.

"One hundred percent true. Ask anyone."

A childlike grin broke Chuck's hard features. He gave a wink then addressed his team, "Let's do this, people. Pike the closest pus-bags while I get Will and his trainees. This is our home, let's keep it clean."

Dillan smiled and whispered, "Thanks, Mom."

Worry crept into his thoughts as he trudged back to the construction site. If the UCs ever evolved into an actual organized force, becoming self-aware or capable of problem-solving, humanity was doomed.

The thought sent his mind spiraling. He started obsessing once again over the resources the community needed to survive. Fall was closing in on them, followed by winter. If it was a typical Northern Ohio winter, they could easily starve to death. How would he keep the water flowing in subzero temperatures? How would he find enough food? The lengthy list of priorities always overwhelmed him. He needed to meet with Pat and Darline. They needed a plan.

He changed direction towards Pat's house when static burst from his radio, followed by Otto's voice. Only he wasn't hailing Dillan, Otto was yelling at Willis.

The transmission was weak, and Dillan strained to hear the exchange. Bits and pieces of the conversation spit through his radio. The transmission cleared enough to run his blood cold.

FST1 was pinned down!

CHAPTER 13
DOUBLE VISION

Randy kicked frantically to free his legs from the grasp of a heavily decayed UC. Putrefied hands held firm to Randy's ACU. Bloodstained hair flailed from its weather-beaten scalp as it struggled to gain control of the food thrashing atop the Hummer. Its milky eyes focused on the meat inches from its mouth.

The level of decomposition identified it as an early victim of the virus, but that didn't stop it from craving human flesh. Parting its festering lips, it darted in for a nibble as Randy slammed his K-Bar through the crown of its moldy skull, sending it to the ground with the blade lodged in its cranium.

His actions bought him a split second to get his body to the center of the vehicle's roof and stand. Randy tried to steady himself as the monsters rocked the enormous Hummer on its springs. He knelt and braced his hands to either side to keep from rolling into the waiting mouths of the dead.

That's when we noticed that he didn't have a gun!

The mass of a dozen UCs had surrounded him. Most of them piled up on the far side of the Hummer, subsequently positioning Randy between them and us and blocking us from firing on the monsters.

"Randy, move that ugly mug of yours. We can't shoot anything," I yelled from the second-story window.

His voice breaking from fear, he said, "I can't, Otto. I'm surrounded. If I flatten out, they'll pull me off."

"What happened to your guns?"

His clipped response spoke to his anxiety, "AR in Hummer, SAW on ground, Glock empty."

"Then you better ask your other question about the Hammer clan, because brother, this doesn't look good for you."

Randy locked me in a nasty glare while Stone gave me a questioning look.

"Don't judge me. He asked the craziest—."

Randy's plea interrupted me. "Do something. I don't want to get eaten!"

"Cover your head. Stone will snipe some UCs and clear a path for you."

Stone's surprised expression prompted me to share my plan.

"Stone, you'll kill the UCs closest to us. That should give Randy room to run to the house. Lisa will kill the UCs on the sides of the Hummer, creating a roadblock for any UCs that break away from the larger group to chase him."

"What are you going to do?" Lisa chirped.

"Well, because I'm seeing double due to my injured head—the injury I sustained while bravely charging the house to save all of you—I'll guard Stripe."

A hard eye-roll preceded Lisa's response, "You were in a blind rage and nearly got yourself killed. If it weren't for Stone, you'd be dead."

"That's your opinion, Lisa. I see it for what it is: I saved you," I said dismissively.

Randy screamed again, refocusing us on the situation at hand: saving him from the UC horde trying to eat him.

Stone reacted by bringing his Tavor online to clear a path for Randy. Lisa shouldered her Sig-MPX and opened up on the UCs on the sides of the Hummer. The maelstrom caused my head to throb and nausea to intensify.

I retreated from the window to cover our prisoner. The sight that greeted me sent fear coursing through my queasy stomach.

Stripe was gone!

CHAPTER 14
THE SHAFTER

The mammoth Yukon plowed through the wreckage of the demolished carport as Shafter stuttered through his conversation with President Wharton.

Banks fumed as Shafter shared more details about the virus. His own government had destroyed the world. He realized that he needed to act, needed to bring them to justice, his personal form of justice!

"That was one heck of a conversation you had with the President," he began after Shafter ended his call. "Which of you idiots thought you could trust North Korea? And who pledged our land to them?"

Shafter feigned fascination with the devastation surrounding them and ignored Banks' question. Finally he glanced at Banks and said, "They really were thorough. Isn't this what you military-types refer to as *scorched earth*?"

"Scribe Shafter, answer my question."

Shafter bristled at the insult but understood the dynamic of the relationship. Without Banks, he wouldn't survive twenty minutes. He swallowed the insult on the tip of his tongue and did as all politicians do. He lied. "I just fed the responsible party to the zombies. I don't think of myself as a hero, although it was a heroic act. I simply did the right thing."

The statement caused Banks to burst into laughter. He glanced at Shafter and said, "Did you just call yourself a hero?" He paused while Shafter fidgeted nervously in the plush leather passenger seat. "That's rich, Scribe Shafter. Thanks for the laugh. I needed it."

Banks cut the wheel hard to the right, slamming into a heavily decomposed monster. The shambling beast's head exploded onto the passenger window, causing Shafter to twist away so violently he nearly snapped his neck while crying out in fear.

"Yep, you're a fearless leader. I'm honored by your presence." Banks course-corrected and aimed the Yukon towards the single opening not blocked by mountains of debris.

"Where to Shafter? Where is Madam President cowering?"

Shaking off the trauma from the collision and resulting insult, Shafter said, "We need to get to San Francisco." He viewed the text from Wharton. "And find a functional shower!"

Banks responded with a hard left turn towards the marina. He reasoned that the fastest way to escape this hellhole was by boat.

"San Fran? You're delusional. We probably won't escape Lemington. We'll never make it to California." Banks paused as he attempted to swerve past a shambling monster, then changed his mind and slammed into it, splattering its head over the Yukon's hood. "Not only would we need to avoid being eaten by zombies, which you helped create ... most of our trek would be across RAM territory. If you haven't noticed, RAM closed their borders. It'd be easier if we were still the United States, but I recall that you instigated the Great Divide. So, what's your plan, genius?"

Banks was already working on a plan that would see them boating to the Maumee River and then to Interstate 80. From that point, it would be a hard-fought battle to reach San Francisco. Actually, it'd be virtually impossible.

But something else was eating at Banks as he swerved the oversized SUV towards the marina. Shafter had divulged all the information about the Coalition's plan, including their North Korean contacts, to Wharton. Why would she need him? President Wharton was in a better position to negotiate with Kim and his minions.

The picture became clear. Shafter was a dead man. She'd said it herself: *Anything tying BSU to this nightmare must be destroyed.* Shafter was the only link tying BSU to the DPRK. She'd ordered him to join her to ensure he was silenced. If the journey didn't kill him, they would execute him upon arrival.

Shafter mumbled a response to Banks' question, but Banks cut him off, "You understand you're a dead man, right?" he asked Shafter as they sped along the trash-filled streets of Lemington. "You're a liability. And you just pissed away the only leverage you held."

Shafter went ashen at the revelation. Banks was right; his value had disappeared the moment he told Wharton about the Coalition's plans. Resignation settling in his voice, he answered, "I suppose you're right." He paused as he searched for a way to escape the mess he'd created. "Do you know anyplace we can go? Someplace we can fortify and hunker down until this blows over?"

Banks gave a sarcastic chuckle before answering, "If I did, I wouldn't have stayed at the Sea Cliff. You unleashed the end of the world, Shafter. You've signed our death warrants."

Banks maneuvered as close to the docks as the huge SUV allowed. Finding a boat wouldn't be a problem; only a small Tri-hull sat moored to the dock. Getting to it would be.

Their arrival attracted the shambling dead from every hole they'd been hiding in and they quickly surrounded the SUV. Banks asked, "Can you operate a boat, or was that a function below your status in life?"

Shafter's response surprised him. "I owned a seventy-foot Bravada X-Series, I think I can handle that tiny Tri-hull."

Banks fixed Shafter with a hard stare and said, "Okay then, let's move." He threw open his door before Shafter could object, taking the keys to the Yukon with him. He'd never trusted politicians and would not let Shafter leave him to die on the dock.

Shafter summoned what little courage he possessed and bolted from the safety of the SUV.

Zombies advanced on him the moment his feet touched pavement. He swung his rebar club wildly, crushing the skull of the closest hungry beast lurching for a bite. More dead filled the void as the first fiend dropped from sight. Again and again, he swung his weapon as his enemies' blood sprayed his howling face.

He searched for Banks amongst the chaos. The gunfire drew his attention to the rear of the Yukon in time to see Banks kill three monsters that had been stalking Shafter from behind. The man had just saved his life.

"Run, Shafter. Run now!" Banks had cleared a quickly disappearing path to the dock, and Shafter shot through it like a greased pig. The hands of the dead tugged on his gore-soaked suit coat as he bobbed-and-weaved toward the boat a mere twenty yards away.

More shots rang out as Shafter willed his legs to move. When he broke free of the ravenous throng, he risked a glance over his shoulder and found Banks blocking the entrance of the narrow dock, rapidly firing on the dead.

"Move, Shafter. I can't hold them off much longer. I'm on my last magazine."

Jumping the last three feet onto the deck of the small boat, he raced frantically to the helm. "No keys!" he screamed.

He searched frantically for the keys and found nothing until he reached under the throttle and came back with a magnetic key holder. He slid it open and found it—the key to his escape. Shafter fumbled with the ignition, then slid the key home and cranked the ignition in one fluid motion. The powerful Mercury outboard motor roared to life as Shafter raced to the boat's stern and lowered the prop into the murky water.

He glanced in Banks' direction and the scene pumped horror through his body. He was battling dozens of monsters as he backed his way towards Shafter. Fear in command, Shafter unmoored the boat, raced back to the helm, and slammed the throttle forward.

He didn't bother to look in Banks' direction as he roared passed him. Shafter rationalized that Banks was already dead as he steered towards the open waters of Lake Erie.

Shock shattered Banks' will to fight when he realized Shafter had sacrificed him to the hungry dead. The same monsters Banks had saved the ruthless bastard from. "Never trust a politician," he smirked.

Acceptance replaced his shock as he watched Shafter fade into the horizon. When gnarled mouths found his flesh, Banks raised his M9 to his temple and pulled the trigger.

CHAPTER 15
THE CAVALRY

I rubbed my eyes but nothing changed. Stripe was still missing. "People, we have a situation," I shouted. Neither Stone nor Lisa heard me over the war they were waging on the UCs trying to eat Randy.

I'd started toward them when their guns fell silent. I figured our plan had worked and expected Randy to enter the house any second until Lisa yelled, "Where are they coming from?"

I rushed to the window, and the sight stole my breath. Dozens more UCs now roamed the street, cutting off Randy's escape and sending him spiraling towards a full-blown panic attack.

"What's happening?" he screamed. "Guys, do something!" His face was red with anxiety and sweat as he scanned the ever-growing crowd surrounding him.

Stone swapped magazines, then stage whispered, "I don't want Randy to hear this, but this is my last mag. We can use the ammo I found in their storage, but it's not enough. Otto, Lisa, what's your ammo situation?"

Lisa answered, "Two mags for my Sig, plus two for my Glock."

"Two for my Ruger, same for my XDm. But we have another problem. Stripe's missing."

Stone's eyes nearly popped from their sockets as the gravity of the situation sank in. "How'd that happen, Otto? Where is he?"

"Oh, I just escorted him to the door and set him free; he's probably in Westlake by now."

Randy's scream stopped Stone from responding or punching me; I'm not sure which, but I'm guessing it was punching me.

"Find him!" he shouted, "and give me one of your magazines."

I tossed him my extra magazine and exited the room as the duo revived their attack on the mob surrounding Randy.

My foggy mind raced. *Where would I hide if I were a terrorist soldier from Blue States United?* I had no answer to the question because I was neither of those things. So I swallowed my nausea and swiftly searched the second floor. Nothing!

Double vision hindered my navigation down the stairs, but Stripe's escape route became apparent when I entered the first floor.

The blacked-out sliders sat ajar, and a small courtyard was visible just beyond. Stripe wanted to make this difficult. He'd pay for doing this to me.

I took one step towards the open sliders when a sound pierced through the clatter of gunfire and rasping dead shambling outside. The sound was unmistakable as its volume grew.

A barrage of gunfire joined the blaring horn causing me to change direction and move to the front door. The cavalry had arrived!

Once outside, I pulled my AR to my shoulder and prepared to rejoin the fight. But the scene stopped me in my tracks. It wasn't Willis' squad coming to our aid.

Jackson's F250 plowed through the UCs like a hot knife through warm butter. Broken bodies scattered like bowling pins as the massive truck asserted its dominance. Full metal jackets split the skulls of any UC lucky enough to have avoided the bone-crushing impact with the truck.

Jackson kept his focus and pulled up beside the Hummer, screaming at Randy to jump into the truck's bed. Randy resembled a gazelle fleeing a lion as he leapt for safety. His landing wasn't as graceful. He slammed to the truck's unforgiving bed and disappeared from sight. Jackson forced his way through the growing herd of walking-rot the instant Randy touched down. He drove to a clearing and maneuvered the truck to face the monsters.

The sights and sounds confused my hazy mind, and the number of UC nightmares had exploded. They started materializing from the left side of the house. The gunfire was too intense to be just Stone and Lisa shooting from the windows above. Then I spotted them: Tesha, Will, and Darline had taken cover behind an abandoned car twenty yards to my right.

I ventured further from the door, waving my arms high and screaming in victory; it touched me that they had risked their lives for us. My gesture was heartfelt, and I wanted them to know I recognized their valiant effort. That's why the cruel response I received—from everyone—bewildered me. I was showing gratitude, people!

"What the hell are you doing, Otto?"

"We can't shoot with your blockhead in the way."

"Move! You idiot." (Lisa).

"Oh my God, Otto. Do you ever pay attention?"

I attempted to match names to insults, but it was no use.

Suddenly my confusion turned to understanding when I spun left and stared directly into the putrid maw of a hideously decomposed UC. *Got it. I just wandered onto the battlefield and blocked everyone's firing lines. And may get myself eaten! I need to work on paying attention!*

In no condition for a fistfight, I ran away; I'll call it a tactical retreat. Jackson's truck was my closest option, but my path quickly flooded with dozens of moldering bodies, and my eyes chose that moment to see double.

I made a hard stop, spun on my heels, and bolted towards the door to the house; it was now blocked by the dead. A split second later, I was scrambling to join the cavalry behind the abandoned car. The screaming faces of the team came into focus when it happened: I found Stripe.

His intent was clear as he charged my friends from their six. He held a large tree branch and locked onto Tesha. I screamed at them to turn around, but they were too busy screaming at me to run. I had one option: take the shot. I slammed to a stop, shouldered my Ruger, and aimed at Stripe.

The stunned expressions on their faces turned to terror as my AR's muzzle waved back and forth trying to determine which image of Stripe to shoot. I watched through my scope as they stopped yelling and dropped from sight behind the car.

Stripe had nearly reached his target as I exhaled and decided I'd shoot both images of the crazed anarchist. I increased the pressure on the trigger while praying that I didn't kill any of my friends. Then Stripe's head disintegrated. His headless carcass stumbled forward a few feet before crumpling to the pavement.

My scope provided an unobstructed view of the pink mist and human particulate hanging in the air and marking the spot where Stripe's head had separated from his body. A flash later, Tesha approached the headless cadaver, her Smith and Wesson 500 Magnum in a two-handed grip leading the way. She had a beautiful AR in dark-earth Cerakote slung across her back.

Will appeared from behind the car, clearly unhappy with what he saw as he frantically flashed a turnaround hand signal. Panic gripped me when I pivoted to find dozens of UCs shambling mere feet behind me. My pathway to safety was quickly disappearing. With Jackson's truck behind my pursuers, I couldn't shoot the monsters, so I grabbed my extendable baton and went to work on putrefied UC skulls.

The baton sliced through the head of the closest UC like a razor-sharp Katana, demonstrating the level of decay my monstrous victim had achieved. Gunfire erupted as the cavalry opened up on the UCs shambling at the fringes while Stone and Lisa attacked the monsters bringing up the rear. I was left to fight my way through the middle of the putrefied mob.

Jackson blared the F250's horn and inched forward; he was making his move and needed the team to cease fire. Their guns fell silent and the truck's engine roared as it exploded through the leading edge of the slimy mass.

Bodies crumpled before the massive truck as it bounced over broken husks, nearly tossing Randy from its bed. I continued to batter the hungry fiends surrounding me, but I risked a glance at the truck plowing through the rotting humanity in its path. Randy's outstretched hand registered, and the plan came into focus. Only one problem. I saw two hands.

With no idea which hand to grab, I swung my baton, wrecking the visage of a cherub-faced UC, reattached the baton to my MOLLE vest, closed my eyes, and thrust my right arm in the air.

My arm felt like it was being ripped from my body when Randy's powerful hand gripped my forearm. On contact, I thrust myself in the same direction that Randy pulled me. When my feet left terra firma, Randy howled in pain but held fast to my arm.

My left hand struggled to grip the truck's bedrails, but it was no use; the slick metal caused my hand to slide away and flail uselessly in the air rushing over me. My boot heels hit pavement, dragging alongside the F250, inches from its knobby rear wheel.

The dead lunged for the meat skidding past them as I attempted to pull myself into the fetal position to avoid having my legs snagged by a fetid hand. Unprepared to support my full weight, Randy slid the length of the truck bed and slammed into the tailgate. His hair-curling shriek told me I was headed for a hard fall.

I closed my eyes, pulled my knees to my chest, and prepared to crash to the street. Suddenly the truck skidded to a hard stop. My momentum carried me forward and forced Randy to lose his grip. White-hot pain filled my vision when my back slapped onto the blacktop. I somersaulted past the cavalry, coming to rest on my back next to Stripe's headless corpse.

Not sure if I'd lived through my *rescue*, I remained perfectly still, pondering the fact that I was a pain in the ass to everyone around me. A dangerous pain, at that. My head drifted to the right, coming face to mutilated neck with Stripe. Jagged skin encircled the gaping hole that once supported his angry head and part of his spine poked from the gaping wound. "Well, you're a sight. Cut yourself shaving, did ya?"

Rapid gunfire, Randy's shrieking, and the sound of a diesel engine approaching combined to shock me to action. I braced for the holy grail of painful experiences and pushed myself to a sitting position. The abundance of road-rash, nicks, cuts, and nausea confirmed that I had survived. The searing pain made me wish I hadn't.

On wobbly legs and fighting the urge to yak, I shuffled towards the truck. Jackson exited and rested a Winchester Model 70 bolt action hunting rifle on the F250's hood. His position would cover us from the approaching diesel-powered vehicle.

The Model 70 is a beautiful and historic weapon that can drive tacks from hundreds of yards, but it's not an ideal choice to fight zombie herds or enemy soldiers. Also, I really didn't appreciate it pointing at my head with Jackson on the trigger. I've seen him shoot a rifle, and unless he took some shooting classes I wasn't aware of, I could easily end up with a bullet in my forehead!

With that thought fresh in my mind, I quickened my pace. I needed to determine why Randy was still screaming, and I figured it'd be better to join him than rejoin the fight. I was a liability on a good day; in my current condition, I'd get everyone killed.

I wasn't prepared for the sight that greeted me when I opened the tailgate. My stomach flipped, and I lurched back. Then a .50 cal began its assault.

CHAPTER 16
VOICE

"Kill her, kill them all. You'll never have this opportunity again."

"No, it's not time. We have much to learn from them."

"Shut up! I say take the shot."

He battled for control as he placed the crosshairs on the head of the woman who'd killed his friend. Winning this round, he slowly panned his Dragunov sniper rifle to the left, finding another target. A familiar-looking old man, shuffling slowly towards the giant truck, presented an interesting option.

"Kill him. They'll assume it was friendly fire. The idiot already blundered into their line of fire once. Kill him."

Herbert was right; this one he could kill with no consequence. But if his timing was off, and the ones battling the monsters heard his shot, they'd find him. He fought the temptation to exterminate the old man. Sweat poured down his face. The salty liquid blurred the vision in his only functioning eye. "It's a sign, Herbert. I'm not supposed to kill him today. We'll track them to their home and slaughter all of them. We'll fulfill our mission."

"NO, we kill them NOW. Give me the gun. You're a coward, just like Williams!"

He held the weapon tight, attempting to shield himself from Herbert's attack. When none came, he spun to face his nemesis but found an empty room. He shot to his feet, calling out to Herbert. There was no reply.

"Where are you? We don't have time for another game of hide-and-seek." Still nothing. "Show yourself. I know you're here. The door's still barricaded. You couldn't have left."

A distant voice reached him and said, *"I'm still here, I'm always here."*

Startled, he took a step towards the door, sending an empty prescription blister-pack skittering across the floor. He didn't remember seeing it before and questioned if Herbert had been holding out on him. His curiosity piqued, he retrieved the package and read the tiny writing on its grimy label. His eyes went wide when the words slammed into his brain. "Clozapine: Dissolve on tongue. Once daily."

Tears streaked his filthy face as he called out, "Herbert Mullin, I need my medication. Please help me find more medication."

CHAPTER 17
ESCALATION

Wharton pressed the end-call button and looked into the stunned faces of the remaining BSU leadership. She grew confused by their lack of enthusiasm. Her confusion shifted to anger when her eyes rested on Nodler and Shank sitting next to her. They were undoubtedly her most unyielding supporters. But today, their glares held contempt.

"What?" she demanded. "This is our only option to regain control of our country." Shank's bulging eyes sent Wharton over the edge she was balancing on. "Do you have a better idea? You've been more concerned with your lodgings than reclaiming our country from the monsters shambling in our streets. So I'm eager to hear your suggestions!"

The group shifted uncomfortably while she glared at them with condemnation.

After a long, uncomfortable silence, Nodler found his voice. "Madam President, we were unaware that a rogue faction of the Blue States United government was responsible for the destruction wrought on our country. Where was your oversight? You're as guilty as the Coalition. In fact, the entire nightmare rests upon your shoulders!"

Wharton responded by unleashing a shrieking diatribe of disjointed babble punctuated by her fist slamming
against Representative Nodler's plump cheek. The blow
sent his eyeglasses spiraling to the yacht's deck, shattering
the left lens. His shock from the assault too great to mount
a counter-attack or even reach for his spectacles, the obese,
vertically challenged politician cowered in his seat, awaiting another blow from the raging Wharton.

The group pulled a collective gasp as Wharton rose
to her feet, screaming her displeasure with them. With a
talon-like finger, she pointed at them and spoke in an icy
tone, "Did you hear what Packet said? They created a cure.
We can stop the spread of the virus and position ourselves
as world saviors!"

Nodler glanced up at the unhinged woman. He
rubbed at his swollen cheek as he addressed her. "Madam
President, you pledged military aid to North Korea. Aid
from a military we no longer possess. What do you think
will happen when they realize you're lying?"

Nodler paused, awaiting another blow from Wharton
for his insubordination.

Her hands trembled as his question sank in. She had
no plan or leverage, no way to lie herself out of the situation. As any true politician would do under these circumstances, she punted responsibility to the morons surrounding her. "The answer to your question will come from the
collective deceitfulness of this group. This war has escalated, and I suggest you commence planning a way for us to

survive. I'll have James guard you while you work. You're all very important, and I wouldn't want anything to happen to you."

Her threat was obvious. James would kill anyone who failed to follow Wharton's direction.

CHAPTER 18
BU GANG

A sickly grin broke on Packet's face; the DPRK would soon rule the Imperial West.

"Packet, you recognize Wharton is lying, do you not?"

His grin never faltering, Packet answered, "I do, Mister Choke. But what a bargaining chip we will possess after we take her, and her ragtag government, into custody. We enjoy the element of surprise. The idiot thinks we are weeks away from arrival. It'll be too late when she realizes I too have a penchant for twisting the truth."

Packet turned to admire the impressive deck of the three-hundred-and-eighty-seven-foot-long *Bu Gang* freighter. His perch on the bridge of the commandeered vessel afforded him a magnificent view of the men and machines that now called the *Bu Gang* home. They scurried about, preparing for the war to come. The scene filled him with pride.

The enormous freighter now towed the remnants of the armada that sailed from Port Namp'o. Packet reveled in the good fortune granted them when they happened upon the mighty freighter while sailing through the Yellow Sea. Commandeering her was child's play, and her crew proved an obedient lot. *Bu Gang*'s meager supplies helped sustain the entire armada during its arduous fifty-five-day journey.

As their warships' fuel ran dry, *Bu Gang*'s massive engines afforded them the ability to attach towlines to the most valuable of the powerless fleet. He'd been sure to secure a Nongo-class missile craft and Nampo-class attack helicopter frigate.

Despite the *Bu Gangs* powerful engines, they were forced to leave many ships adrift in the Pacific Ocean; Packet viewed it as an unavoidable sacrifice for the greater good. Most crew members from those abandoned ships found shelter aboard the *Bu Gang*. Those left behind received promises of a rescue that Packet had no intention of providing. They were the weakest among them and would only sap his dwindling resources.

China had retaliated more quickly than expected, destroying most of North Korea's military assets along the Sea of Japan, including its entire fleet of submarines.

Packet now viewed the devastation as a blessing. The reduced fleet size helped them avoid being detected by Right America's mighty Seventh Fleet. *A Brown Water Navy outmaneuvered the most devastating military force on the planet*, Packet mused.

Choke's voice broke through the victorious images playing in Packet's mind. "Vice Chair Packet, are you listening? We possess little time to plan our invasion."

Annoyed by the intrusion into his visions, Packet's response dripped with disdain. "I'm always listening, Choke. Watch your tone, or you'll find yourself swimming to shore." He turned to face Choke and locked eyes with him, then barked, "SPEAK, Choke. What is your grand vision for our victory?"

Choke bowed his head from instinct, not respect, and cursed himself for doing so. Regaining his composure, he lifted his chin towards the snake of a man and said, "As I stated, we have little time to prepare for an invasion of this magnitude. We will reach San Francisco ..."

Choke was cut short by the ship's captain. "Land in sight, awaiting orders."

Without hesitation, Packet replied, "Enter San Francisco Bay!"

CHAPTER 19
DISLOCATION

Dozens of .50 cal rounds buzzed overhead, prompting me to take cover in the truck's bed. Randy howled in pain while writhing like a hooked worm. I couldn't bear to look at him and didn't dare leave the safety of the truck. I was trapped!

With the tailgate down, I decided to watch the show instead of dealing with Randy. The big gun laid waste to the UC horde shuffling in our direction. Moldering bodies were torn apart as the 709-grain full-metal-jacketed rounds found their flesh-covered targets. The Ma-Duce was quickly joined by the unmistakable sound of an M249 spitting her M855 rounds into the unlucky monsters at the rear of the mass.

I was content to hunker down and enjoy the raw display of military power. But Randy's pleas managed to rise above the ear-splitting cacophony of fully automatic weapons. He was committed to ruining the show for me!

"Otto, I need your help."

"Randy, I can't even look at you. How do you expect me to help you?"

"OTTO, this happened while I was saving your sorry ass. Now get over here and HELP ME."

It's always about him, I thought as I prepared myself for the *events* to follow. "Okay, I'm coming over. But I don't know how to fix that mess you've got going on. You may die."

"Otto, we have killed countless UCs, not to mention living humans. We've seen things that will haunt us for the rest of our lives. But my dislocated shoulder is TOO MUCH for your delicate sensibilities?"

He had a point, but he obviously hadn't taken a peek at himself. His arm hung down about four inches while flopping around like a fish out of water. I knew what he wanted me to do, and it was making my stomach queasier than my concussed head already had.

I kept my body flat to the bed, my head down, and squirmed my way to him. "What's next? Remember, I'm not a medic."

"You need to pop it into its socket. And, once you start, don't stop. If you stop, I will punch you."

To do what Randy asked meant two things would happen: I'd have to look at his shoulder and touch his flailing arm. "Yah, I'm not going to be able to do that. Come at me with a better idea."

"OTTO, we need to get it back into place before it swells like a balloon. If we wait too long, I'll need surgery to fix it. DO IT NOW!"

"Okay, okay. Relax, man, I'll handle it. You need to turn so I can get leverage." I was stalling because I had no clue how to proceed. It didn't work. In less than a second,

Randy had spun around, placed his feet on the bedrails, and ordered me to fix him.

I swallowed hard as bile rose into my throat. I grabbed his limp appendage, rotating it to a ninety-degree angle to his body. His howling response caused me to flinch and yank on his arm, subsequently sending him over the edge.

His left arm rose with his hand forming a tight fist. I shut my eyes and waited to get pummeled. Instead, he screamed, "What's wrong with you, Otto? Are you trying to kill me? Do you have any compassion?" It was impressive how clearly his voice pierced the battle raging around us.

With Randy's fury distracting him, I figured the time to act had arrived. I prayed that all the movies were accurate and quickly pulled on his arm. The rolling, grinding, and popping sensation from the damaged joint made me woozy. Inky clouds filled my vision, and I rolled onto my back, pulling deep breaths to fight against my mind's desire to shut down.

Sweat saturated my body, but the fear of being harassed for passing out spurred me to action. I sat up and shook off the urge to succumb to my body's request to quit.

Suddenly, a UC head landed hard against my thigh, snapping me back to reality. The body that belonged to the head stood motionless at the tailgate before crumbling to the blacktop. The UC had been seconds from feasting on my hide before its head was skillfully removed.

I glanced at the molting head to find its putrid maw working up and down, attempting to sate the unrelenting hunger driving it to devour human flesh. Shocked, I kicked it from the truck and turned to search for the person responsible for saving my life.

I expected to see Will or maybe Darline standing in a haze of gun smoke, displaying a look of grim satisfaction with exterminating the monster. That was before I heard Jackson's triumphant whooping!

No shit, he took shooting lessons. I broke the thought to yell my thanks when the first of two Hummers roared between us, blocking my view, the second close behind. The beefy machines churned through the field of shattered bodies while speeding to the side of the house where this disastrous mission began. The war machines pulled side by side, then the .50 cal came online, sending an unrelenting stream of copper-jacketed death into an unseen enemy.

I turned back to thank Jackson and found his face inches from my own.

"Jesus, Jackson. You scared the crap out of me. Let a guy know when you're creeping up on him. You're lucky I didn't shoot you."

Worry creased Jackson's features. His eyes searched the length of my body, then locked me in an unblinking stare. "You feeling okay, Otto?" Before I could answer, he shifted his gaze to an unmoving Randy. "What happened to Randy?" His voice was strained, and he stepped backwards as he spoke.

I realized what was happening when the others came into view. They positioned themselves behind Jackson with guns at low ready. Darline gave me a tight grin.

"Whoa there, people, how 'bout you check your guns at the door. We weren't bitten."

"Otto, what happened to Randy? He was screaming and flailing around, and we saw the top of your head by him. So, what happened?"

The intensity in Jackson's voice put me on edge. I searched out Darline and found her looking intense and ready for action. "Really, babe? You're just falling in line with my homicidal brother? We'll talk later!"

Jackson relaxed after I questioned Darline's willingness to kill me. "He's fine!" he shouted over his shoulder.

"Well, I'm alive. Not sure about fine," I shot back.

Randy finally quit his *I'm dead because Otto killed me* act and said, "No, he's not *fine*. You should put him down like a dirty dog."

"Hey, Randy. A little gratitude for my valiant efforts would be nice. You'd still be crying like a girl if it wasn't for me."

The group started toward the truck the same instant the Ma-Deuce ceased fire. The silence was deafening and prompted the group to look in the Hummers' direction. An unfamiliar face barked an all-clear from the turret while scanning the area for threats.

The door to the house opened slowly, and a pole with a filth-covered white tee-shirt emerged. Lisa's nerve-crackled voice rang out. "We're coming out, and we're friendly. Don't shoot."

The turret gunner locked onto the movement and prepared to fire. His action prompted me to slide from the truck bed. When my feet hit pavement, my knees buckled, nearly sending me to the ground. I leaned back, bracing myself against the tailgate while screaming, "He's friendly. Don't shoot my brother."

An angry voice bellowed from the darkened doorway, "I will whoop you, Otto Hammer."

"Oh, Lisa, you're such a kidder."

Everyone paused while waiting for Stone and Lisa to exit the building. When nothing happened, I added, "Lisa's okay too."

The soldier quickly spun Ma-Deuce in our direction and, with fury blazing in his eyes, opened fire.

CHAPTER 20
CHATTER

"They are killing your forces. Shoot them!"

"Welcome back, Herbert. Are you going to help me find more medication?"

"I've told you a hundred times, you don't need medication. It clouds your thoughts and slows you down. Besides, you're more fun when you don't take it."

"I'm reckless when I don't take my medication and people die. People we need right now are rotting away in an abandoned store while we struggle to complete our mission."

"Shut up and shoot. Kill the soldier firing the turret gun first. Then shoot the familiar-looking old man."

"NOOOO! Shut your mouth! Your chatter drives me crazy. It echoes around my head, making it impossible to concentrate."

He knew he should kill the terrorists invading his camp. But doing so didn't support the mission. Killing their entire community was his primary objective, and he was determined to complete that assignment.

"Now, I understand why you lost your eye. You wouldn't listen and somebody finally had enough of your bullheadedness and

poked it out! By the way, that patch covering your empty socket makes you look like a pirate."

"Herbert, I'm numb to your schoolyard insults."

He didn't wait for Herbert's retort; he knew what he needed to do. On his feet a moment later, he attacked the barrier blocking the door, tossing chairs and boxes aside. He hesitated when he reached the heavy oak dresser.

"Herbert, can you show me how you're constantly escaping from the room without moving the barrier?" When Herbert didn't reply, he searched the room for the bane of his existence and found himself alone … again.

Frustrated, he pushed hard against the mammoth piece of furniture, his effort futile against its heavy oak construction. "Capitalism strikes again!" he cursed. "Who needs this much storage? Oh, I remember, a capitalist pig, that's who. Just buy more and more stuff; then you simply buy something to store all of your worthless treasures in. This is a microcosm of why I hate RAM."

The thought caused anger to explode through his body, releasing gallons of adrenalin into his raging system and blinding him to his actions. When his mind calmed, the sight greeting him brought a smile to his face. The weighty oak monument to excess was now just a broken heap of splinters strewn about the room.

After admiring his work, he bolted down the staircase and through the rear exit of the commandeered house. He rushed across the yard and easily scaled the six-foot-high privacy fence separating him from his first stop.

Two forty-by-ten CONEX containers rested side by side, concealed under a large woodland-camouflaged tarp. He thrust the locking handle up, releasing the cam and freeing the door to swing open. The stench of rotting human flesh blasted his senses, forcing him to stumble back. He recovered and sprinted to the neighboring container and freed its inhabitants.

He positioned himself in front of the cavernous metal boxes and waved his arms while screaming, "My soldiers, now is the time. Follow me to victory." He watched spellbound as his army of festering corpses emerged from their CONEX barracks. Driven by insatiable hunger, they marched towards their leader by the hundreds.

Satisfied that he held their attention, he jogged to the front of the house and peered around the corner. The battle waged on only twenty-five yards away. He glanced over his shoulder and found the first of his troops within biting range. He bolted from cover en route to the next set of *barracks* across the street, which housed additional troops.

When his boots slapped pavement, the pandemonium of war ceased. Panic overrode his instinct to immediately seek cover and propelled him forward.

When he reached safety between two abandoned homes, the terrorists' guns came back online. He slammed to a stop and turned to face his army and watched in horror as they were slaughtered like animals.

"I told you to kill them. The terrorists have destroyed your troops!"

CHAPTER 21
NEW GUY

"Have you lost your mind? Did serving under Sergeant Willis send you over the edge? That's it. Willis made you crazy! That explains it!" I had pulled into the fetal position under the F250, screaming at the new guy in Willis' squad. And I was nowhere near finished.

"Sergeant Willis, can you explain to, to ... what's your name, soldier?"

The befuddled soldier answered, "Andrews, Sir. Private Andrews. Can I ask why you're so whacked out of shape? I just saved you."

"For God's sake, you pointed that big-ass gun at us and fired it. I thought you'd gone rogue. A little warning would've been nice!"

"I knew what he was doing." - Jackson

"Me too." - Tesha

"Otto, you did the same thing to us five minutes ago." - Will

"Otto, STOP IT." - Darline

Still in the fetal position and safely hidden under the truck, I launched my counterattack.

"I quit. That's right, you heard me. I'm finished with you ungrateful people. Jackson can take my place on FST1.

Good luck with that, he can't shoot. Oh, and hopefully you'll treat him better if he gets concussed while heroically trying to save you. If he'd even try to save you, that is." (Dramatic pause) "Why so quiet? Trying to figure out how you'll make it without me? Well, toooo bad, you can't talk me out of it. You're on your own now, losers!"

I geared up for round two when boots suddenly appeared in front of me. "Otto, everyone's loading up. So, unless you want to walk home with your *concussed* head, zip it and join us." The voice belonged to Willis, and he obviously found amusement with my distress.

"Willis, is everyone staring at us?"

"Yep."

"Then I'll stay here."

"Can't let you do that, Otto."

"But I don't feel good, and I'm comfortable."

"Suck it up, Otto. We gotta go."

My pride dented, I wiggled from under the truck and struggled to my feet. I searched for, and found, Andrews' smirking face staring back at me. I swallowed a string of insults I had prepared and opted to let him know that I was *onto him*. I have no idea what exactly I was onto, but I was indeed onto it. My pointer and middle fingers forming a "V," I pointed to my eyes then jabbed my fingers at him. Andrews' laughter confirmed that he didn't care. *He's on my list!*

Willis' eyes bugged when he saw my face. "Jesus, Otto. What happened? You look like hell."

I didn't realize that concussions were visible to the naked eye, and my expression telegraphed my confusion.

"Your face, Otto. It's a bloody mess. What happened?"

I had forgotten all about my wounded face. "I was shot, Willis. Shot in the face trying to save my friends and loved ones."

Lisa and Stone joined us as I finished proclaiming myself a martyr. I put my best puppy dog eyes on full display as I waited for my team to rally around me. Then Lisa spoke. Well, first she laughed, then she spoke. "Oh, for the love of God. You weren't shot, Otto. Your tender little face got grazed by some metal shards."

That did it. I refused to be insulted one more time. I'd been through enough already. I stormed past my *friends*, including my wife, slid through the open crew door, into the backseat of Jackson's truck, and slammed the door. Sitting perfectly still, I stared at the headrest in front of me. I was never going to talk to these people again.

Darline helped Randy get into the truck while he groaned like a man entering his death throes. I was convinced he was faking. I geared up to tell him how I felt about his performance when his door shut, and his suffering ceased. When I glanced at him, his face displayed a wide grin, and he winked at me.

I sucked in a prodigious amount of air to accommodate the litany of profanity I intended to share with him. However, when Jackson and Darline climbed into the cab, he started groaning and rocking his head from side to side. It hit me. He was setting me up, egging me on and trying to get me to yell at the *poor wounded Randy* so I'd look like a bigger jerk than I already did. Not today, Kemosabe, not today! Biting my tongue, I did the next best thing and flipped him the bird!

The ride home was quiet except for Randy's *suffering*. When we pulled to the gate, I asked, "Did Willis drop off the food and HAM radio he owes us for helping with yet another poorly planned mission?"

Darline turned in her seat to face me. "The truck arrived at the gate around the same time Dillan radioed that you needed backup. So I'm assuming the MREs and radio are now stored away in the community pantry."

"Good. I also need to talk to him. I'm going to ask for a helmet; I'd be fine if I had one on when I hit the door."

"Oh, that's how you got *concussed*. You slammed your noggin into a door. I can't wait to hear that story." Darline paused while shaking her head, then continued, "Well, you better move quickly because he's going to Camp Hopkins after they drop off the others."

Randy put his suffering on hold long enough to interject, "We have helmets, Otto. You hate wearing yours. Be smarter next time; be like me and wear a helmet."

My head snapped in Randy's direction so quickly my vision blurred and caused a wave of nausea so intense I gagged.

Before I could recover, Jackson yelled, "Don't you dare throw up in my truck." Then he rolled my window down. "Out the window, man, hang your sick head out the window!"

I swallowed hard, tried to regain my composure, and blurted out, "I was also shot in the face by a bullet."

"Shrapnel hit you. Not a bullet."

"You seem to have recovered quickly from your injury, Randy. How d'you manage that?"

Randy immediately fell back into character, groaning louder than ever.

"That's what I thought. Jerk!"

Darline interjected. "Stop it, both of you. Otto, we'll talk later. Randy, we're not buying your act. We'll have Durrell and Sabrina check you two over and get you home. But for now, please remain silent. You're making me cranky."

"Jack, get me to the clinic before I bleed out. You know, because I've been SHOT!"

CHAPTER 20
HUMAN TRIALS

One thing the government got right was assigning military units to RAM's hospitals immediately after they identified the virulence level of the virus. The country still lost dozens of medical facilities and hundreds more hospital staff. Mercifully, they salvaged the vast majority of RAM's medical infrastructure.

The military code-named the offensive "Operation Nightingale," but it bore no resemblance to its namesake. It proved to be a vicious and bloody operation which forced impossible choices on confused young soldiers—choices whose scars lived on in the eyes of every person involved with the campaign.

After the military commandeered Saint Joe's Hospital, they relocated any patients not suffering from a terminal illness to an adjacent medical office building providing basic care to a lucky few.

Over the following weeks, the military erected dozens of military mobile hospital units on the sprawling grounds of Saint Joe's, swelling its capacity to three thousand beds. But even at that size, it continued to struggle through one hundred percent capacity.

Eventually, the flow of sick and injured citizens had slowed to a trickle. Word quickly spread of the hospital's harsh protocols surrounding infected persons arriving at its gates. If you were infected, you were humanely terminated, which wasn't an issue; everyone understood that the infected needed to be destroyed. However, if you even *looked* infected, you were humanely terminated. If hospital staff couldn't identify your illness, you were humanely terminated. It escalated to where if you even appeared nervous about being tested, you were humanely terminated. Those protocols kept the sick away and cost hundreds of people their lives. But they also allowed the hospital to regain control, in turn, allowing them to focus on studying the virus in hopes of developing a cure.

Ben

Nurse Jenkins held tight to Benjamin Reyes' trembling hand while he waited for Doctor McCune to begin the treatment. He glanced up and met her compassionate stare. They had grown close during his time at Saint Joe's. Both had lost their families to the virus and found solace in one another's stories of life before the world ended.

Now, she would watch him risk death to help save humanity.

Ben tried to comfort his friend. "It's the right thing to do, Ann. We both know I don't have much time left."

Ann's breath hitched when Ben spoke. She knew his cancer was winning and could take him at any moment. But his words still rocked her emotions.

"Thank you, Ann. Thank you for being a friend."

With wet eyes, she bent down and kissed his forehead. "I'll see you in a few hours."

McCune stepped from behind the privacy curtain and asked, "Ben, are you ready to begin?"

Ben answered with a stiff nod. He closed his eyes and tried to envision the smiling faces of his family. The thought brought a grin to his face.

"Excellent. And Ben, thank you." Doctor McCune slid the needle into the IV bag's medicine port and pressed the plunger. "We don't know if this will be painful and I'm sorry we can't administer a sedative, Ben. The virus' interaction with opiates is quite volatile."

McCune glanced down and found Ben asleep. He breathed a sigh of relief at the sight. *At least it isn't painful.* "Nurse Jenkins, you should leave. We're unsure of how the antidote will react in the living. It could be violent."

Jenkins looked at her friend one last time and left. The legions of armed soldiers standing guard confirmed the doctor's concerns. The unknown could prove deadly in today's reality. She quickened her pace, her fear becoming so great she worried she may faint.

McCune observed Ben for fifteen minutes, carefully noting his vital signs and scribbling notes at even the slightest change. He felt hope building. Ben's vitals had normalized. In fact, they appeared stronger than before he'd administered the antidote. If it didn't kill his uninfected test subjects, they'd be able to move forward with aerosolizing the cure.

McCune turned away from Ben and walked into the isolation ward. He met the anxious stares of dozens of doctors and nurses and said, "Proceed with administering the antidote. Our human trials have begun."

An hour later, two hundred doses had been administered.

CHAPTER 21
CHARLEY FOXTROT

Dread's icy hands gripped Sergeant Willis. His chest felt tight, and his heart thumped in his ears. He pressed the radio's talk button and said, "Say again, Lewis."

"We identified the headless enemy as Dexter Hump. We identified the combatant in the house as Aden Hump, over." After a pause, Lewis said, "Sergeant, we have no Bobby Smith on site. Awaiting orders."

"Find a hole. I'm reporting to Albright, over."

Willis shoved his knuckles into his eyes before he radioed Albright. His frustration would control his mouth if he didn't wait for it to simmer down. After a ten-count, he switched to Camp Hopkins' channel and spoke. "Willis for Hopkins, how copy?"

"Hopkins has a good copy on Sergeant Willis, over."

"Hopkins, I need Albright on the line ASAP, over."

"Roger that; hold for Albright."

Willis watched sixty seconds tick away on his G-Shock. His patience had begun slipping away when the radio finally crackled with Albright's voice. "Go for Albright."

Choosing not to address Albright by rank or name, Willis said, "We are negative on Bobby Smith."

"Any INTEL on where he squirted to? Over."

"Negative. We completed a house to house of the immediate area. Bobby Smith is a ghost. Albright, one more thing. We found seven CONEX trailers, all open, and all held UCs at some point, over."

Albright understood his meaning. Hundreds of UCs, possibly thousands, had been released into the streets. Through a clenched jaw, he asked, "Do you have a visual on force size? Over."

"Negative. We engaged several hundred the other day and roughly two dozen when we returned today. Our recon found large, recently trampled paths through the surrounding brush. Our observation is that hundreds are now roaming the city, over."

Albright let the information percolate before responding. "Sergeant, regroup at Hopkins. We'll send a Shadow up to recon the area." After a long pause, he continued, "Willis. Report directly to me when you arrive at Hopkins. We need to talk. Albright, out."

CHAPTER 22
CONVALESCING

"There's a lot to do, Randy. It's overwhelming; it keeps me up at night."

"Me too, Otto. We'll be knee-deep in snow before long."

"Yep, it's almost flannel shirt season. However, it's time for our walk with Tesha's little guy; we'll finish solving the world's problems later."

"You don't remember his name, do you?"

"Nope."

"Good to see your concussion didn't change you, Otto."

"I'm still solid as a rock."

Five days had passed since our last mission. My headache was finally coming under control, and my vision had stopped doubling. But I needed a break, so I decided to follow Durrell's advice: rest and avoid slamming my head against hard objects.

Randy wasn't as fortunate. His arm was in an immobilizing sling, and he wasn't happy about it. Nor was his wife. An hour into day one of recuperating, Nila ordered him out of their home. Now he visits me every day. And, well, here we are, hiding from our wives while we convalesce.

I couldn't stomach sitting still with him for more than an hour, so we started taking Tesha's son with us while we helped manage the teams that Dillan built. My favorite was the gun cleaners; I think they truly appreciated my insight into the art of cleaning a weapon.

We pulled our aging bodies from the Adirondack chairs on my front porch and headed towards Tesha's.

"Are you really quitting, Otto?"

"Quitting what?"

"Don't play games; you know what I'm talking about."

I knew what he meant, and I wanted to avoid the conversation. It wasn't a simple decision. Even after my temper-tantrum five days ago, it wasn't easy. I was a liability on our missions. With the attention span of a five-year-old at an amusement park, I would eventually get someone killed.

"Don't make this an issue, okay? I'm taking a step back to evaluate my role on the team before someone dies. I'm not going all teary-eyed Rick Grimes on you, just taking a breather. Andy can take my place. I hear he's eager to join FST1, so give him a chance."

Randy's response was cut off by an excited voice emanating from Tesha's front yard. "Mister Otto, Mister Randy, Mom said I can go with you guys, but she wants to talk to you. I think you're in trouble." Then he spun and barreled into the house.

"Randy, what's the kid's name?"

His reply was a snorting laugh.

"Thanks, Randy, you're a *good* friend."

Tesha's front door held some terrible memories for me, and I stood at the exact spot where she'd nearly ended my life. In no hurry to repeat history, I called to her through the screen door.

"I won't shoot you, Otto. You're safe, come in," she said while chuckling at my apprehension.

Her son was ready to go; he had slipped his backpack on and held his notepad at the ready. I kneeled and asked, "So, little man. Who do we visit first?"

Without missing a beat, he said, "The dumbass teen-agers cleaning the guns."

Tesha wasn't thrilled. "DEVON, watch your mouth. Who taught you that word?"

I already knew Devon's answer, and now I remembered his name. So, I closed my eyes and waited for it.

"Sorry, Mom. That's what Mister Otto called them. He said they're doing a lousy job." Pointing to his notepad, he continued, "Look at all their vio, err vala, um venat—"

"Violations," I interjected.

"Huh, is that so? Mister Otto is teaching you curse words. Devon, go pick up your school books and put them away. I need to talk to Mister Otto and Mister Randy."

Devon sulked by us and whispered, "Told you. You're in trouble."

After Devon cleared earshot, I went for a preemptive strike, "Tesha, I'm sorry. My mouth moves faster than my brain. I'll be more careful with Devon around."

Tesha breathed deep and said, "Otto, Randy, we need to talk. Grab a seat."

Chapter 23
Field Guidance

"Darline, he needs to stop. Do whatever you need to do, just please make him stop."

Al waited until Randy and Otto left for their afternoon walk before swooping in to talk to Darline. Twenty minutes later, he was still pleading with her for help.

"How much longer until that damned head of his heals? We'll have a full-blown mutiny if he keeps this up."

Darline felt bad for Al but not bad enough to force Otto to stay home all day. He would literally drive her crazy.

"Al, what can I do? Otto's a grown man, I can't ground him."

"Give him some chores to do. Don't wake him up in the morning. Do something!"

"Al, it can't be that bad."

Al's eyes nearly shot from their sockets. He stuttered and stammered as he ran through all the things Otto had done. Calming down enough to speak clearly, he said, "Darline, he visits every team EVERY DAY. He brings his little ... mini-me and Randy with him. Then he inspects everything the teams are doing. He had the nerve to run a white cloth over the guns the kids just finished cleaning, checking for dirt. A WHITE GLOVE INSPECTION is what it was. The teams started calling it *Field Guidance.* And they call him *Mister Kim!*"

The revelation didn't surprise Darline. Otto obsessed over clean guns. She'd heard him preach about it for years. *A clean gun is a reliable gun.* She smiled because she knew that's the lecture the youngsters were hearing.

Al paced back and forth in front of Darline, waving his hands and ranting. She'd tuned him out until he mentioned Otto rejoining FST1. She didn't have the heart to tell him that Otto might quit the team. Actually, she feared Al would blow a gasket and die in her living room. Instead, she lied. "I'll talk to him, Al. I'm sure he'll understand."

Chapter 24
Bend The Rules

The room was pin-drop quiet when Tesha finished. The awkward silence felt hours long. She ran out of patience and said, "Will one of you please talk! You're creeping me out with your bug-eyed stares."

Her statement pulled me from my stupor, and I responded as I often do in these situations. I rambled. "Tesha, you can't join FST1; it's against the rules. You need to think about Devon. Who'll take your place on the security detail? Did you talk to your sister? Is she prepared to raise Devon if you get killed? You saw how dangerous it can be. Are you ready for that? I can't …"

Tesha brought my rant to an abrupt end when she made a timeout signal with her hands and yelled, "Stop, timeout, cool your jets, Otto. Do you think I'm taking this lightly? Like I haven't considered all the things you just rambled endlessly about?"

She locked me in a hard stare before continuing. "Your response shows I wasn't clear. So I'll simplify it for you. I'm joining FST1. I need to keep my family safe. And the best way to do that is by stopping threats before they reach our gates. Bend the rules, Otto. I'll show up for training at 0700 tomorrow. Inform FST1 I'm its newest member."

I started to protest when Randy undermined my argument, "Okay, you're now part of FST1. It's a good time to expand the team; you'll be a solid addition."

"What the hell, Randy?"

"Hey, you're quitting the team. You have no say. Plus, we need to keep the team fresh, possibly set up a revolving member system. It also gives us the ability to dispatch multiple teams to different areas simultaneously. Honestly, we should recruit even more members."

It was apparent the news of my departure from FST1 surprised Tesha. But she didn't comment. Instead, she chose to cut the conversation short by yelling, "Devon, it's time to go."

A smiling Devon rumbled into the room half a second later and said, "Let's go take care of those dumba—. Um, those teenagers. They need *so* much help."

He grabbed my hand and pulled until I relented and stood to join him for our daily inspections.

When we got to the street, I asked Devon to cover his ears; he looked up at me like only a five-year-old can and said, "I'm supposed to always hold your hand. I can't cover my ears and hold your hand at the same time."

KIDS! "It'll be okay for a minute, and only this time. I need to talk to Mister Randy about grownup things."

With a sly grin, he looked at Randy and said, "Mister Randy. You're in trouble."

Devon handed me his notepad and plugged his ears.

"What the hell, Randy? We can't let that happen."

Randy ignored my indignation. He looked at Devon and said, "My second question was, why no kids in the Hammer clan?"

I slammed to a stop and spun to face him. "What? Are you damaged in a way I haven't noticed?"

"That's the second question I had for you when I thought we were going to die. So spill it. Why no kids?"

He had me so rattled I couldn't think straight. I contemplated punching him. When I started to reply, he held up his hand. "I can see why Darline wouldn't want a bunch of tiny Otto's running around. But none of you have kids. Why? Is it a genetic thing, or are you just shooting blanks?"

Red-faced and near ready to follow through on punching him, I yelled, "You sound like my mom! You want to know why? Kids are expensive!"

I turned from his shocked face, grabbed Devon's hand, and stomped away, yelling, "It's time for inspections, jerk!"

CHAPTER 25
CROSSHAIRS

"Shoot the boy, then the old man."

"Herbert, stop talking and go find my medication. I'll act when it's time."

"The time is now. Shoot the child."

He placed the crosshairs on the boy's head. From this distance, his Russian-built Dragunov would easily remove the child's head. His finger hovered over the Dragunov's trigger as he chewed his bottom lip, fighting the impulse to initiate the war.

"No, Herbert. Our troops are marching our way as we speak. Hundreds more wait for us to release them. We will finish our mission."

"You are weak, a coward. Afraid to kill an enemy child even as millions of our children have been slaughtered by the scourge RAM set loose upon us. I pray you live forever so you can relive your failures every day for eternity."

"Herbert, if you speak again, I will feed you to our hungry soldiers. You'll serve as an appetizer before they devour this homestead."

He felt Herbert's frosty stare on his neck. Spinning sharply to meet the glare of his archenemy, he found the man had once again fled.

"You won't even stay to fight! Who's the coward?"

From a distant point in the derelict home that served as their base camp, a voice answered him, *"No, Bobby Smith! You are the coward."*

CHAPTER 26
INTERVENTION

We finished our inspections in record time, so I split from Devon and Randy early. I wasn't sure if it was my mood or a fact. But it seemed the teams were regressing. The thought added to my salty mood. *They aren't listening. I need to talk to Dillan and Al. They're being too soft.*

With everything that had happened during the day, my worry and anger boiled over as I stomped home. I needed to vent before my head exploded. *Sorry, Darline. Today's your unlucky day!*

I slammed the door and stopped cold at the sight that greeted me. Al, Dillan, Lisa, Will, and Tesha sat in my living room.

"DARLINE, why are people in our home? I'm in no mood for company!"

Her answer just plain sucked. "I'm upstairs. This is an intervention. Grab a seat; it could be a long afternoon."

"Whose intervention? And why are we intervening?"

Lisa answered the question I had specifically asked of Darline. "It's your intervention, Otto. You've become more irrational than ever. We're concerned you've slipped over the edge, you know, gone completely crazy. That thick skull of yours has taken a lot of abuse, and it finally broke."

"Darline, why is Demon-Breath talking?" I said while lurching in the she-devil's direction.

Darline suddenly appeared in front of me, halting my forward progress. She locked eyes with me and yelled, "Not helpful, Lisa."

Lisa spoke between chortles, "I know, but it's funny. You should see your face, Otto. You look as crazy as we think you are."

I leaned close to Darline and, barely above a whisper, asked, "What's happening?"

"We can hear you, Otto."

"Lisa, I'm speaking to my wife. If I wanted to hear your wretched voice, I'd direct my question to Lucifer!"

Instead of answering, Darline joined the intervention gang and asked me to sit and listen. Instead, I took a mock count of the people assembled around me and asked, "Only six of you? You may need backup." I grabbed my radio and said, "I can call Pat, do you want me to call Pat? She'll be a wonderful addition to your little ambush!"

Darline's response momentarily derailed my coun-terattack. "Pat is with Bill Jenkins' wife helping with Bill's physical therapy."

I had forgotten about Bill and cringed at my oversight. Cringed, yes. Did it knock the fight out of me? No!

"Well, my brothers are probably free. I can radio them. Because I'm confident you're going to need help!"

"Otto, just sit and listen. We're not going to *attack* you. Your friends and I want to talk, that's all. Just talk," Darline said while motioning to the group.

"What?" Lisa started. "I'm here to attack him. He's being bullheaded and difficult. We find it very ... shall I say, *triggering*."

That word! The single most destructive word in the English language. It's designed to shut you down, make you feel sorry for the *triggered* person. It doesn't matter if what you're saying is accurate. Nope, if you trigger them, you must be silent. On most occasions, I call bullshit! But this time I considered the source. Lisa was baiting me. She wanted me to lose what little control I had left. Not today, Beelzebub!

"Well, in that case, I'll take a seat." I plopped down and continued, "We can't upset the snowflakes in the house, so I'll shut my face and listen."

Lisa flinched at my jab, causing Dillan to grab hold of her left hand, keeping her on the couch. Her menacing stare told me she'd be seeking revenge; my counter-stare told her to bring it!

Darline pulled us back to the subject at hand: me and my *behavior*. "Okay, now that we've gotten that out of our systems. Let's get started." She glanced at our *guests* with an anticipatory gaze. Finally, she said, "Anyone? You all had a lot of opinions and complaints when Otto wasn't around. So, let's share them with the source of your angst."

Nervous stares and fidgety humans greeted me, but no one vocalized their concerns. I geared up to proclaim victory when Al broke through his indecision. He was not pleasant. "You're driving us crazy, Otto. The teams are threatening to quit because of you. Please stop your inspections. They call it field guidance like we live in North Korea."

He'd caught me off guard, but he was clearly mistaken. "Al, the kids appreciate my input and you know it. Anyway, if the teams were doing a better job, the inspections would be nothing more than a social visit. But holy smokes, man. What they consider a clean gun is sad."

Other than Randy, I've never seen a human turn the deep red that Al's face achieved. I was impressed with both my ability to elicit such an intense reaction and with Al's body's ability to push that much blood into his face. Veins that hadn't carried blood in years bulged from his forehead while he stammered his response, "We are not cleaning our weapons for use by the Silent Drill Team, Otto. No one can live up to your *clean gun* standards."

He had a point, but I was under attack, so I countered, "A clean gun is a reliable gun." I quickly shifted the argument. "What about the ammo team? I've never ..."

Somehow Al's face turned a deeper shade of red. "You told them to clean the spent brass twice. Then you directed them to weigh every single load. EVERY. SINGLE. LOAD! Otto, we produce over a thousand rounds a day. Your *guidance* is insane, just like you!"

I was losing the argument, so I employed my famous re-direction tactic, "Give me the load data for your 9mm reloads and I'll back off." I'd been trying to get Al's 9mm load data for years, but he acted like a little old lady with a blue ribbon carrot cake recipe.

Al settled back on the couch and squinted his eyes, ending the conversation with an emphatic, "Over my dead body! I'm locking the doors. You no longer have access to the teams, Otto Hammer!" With that, he stood and stormed from the house.

"Who's next?" I asked.

Will spoke. "Hey, I'm just here to collect your gear. Tesha told me she's taking your place on FST1. She begins training tomorrow, so we need your gear."

I was taken aback that Will wasn't a little more concerned about my departure, and I'd never considered that I'd be giving up my toys when I quit. But I couldn't argue, so just above a whisper I said, "My gear is upstairs. I'll go get it."

Darline sprang to her feet and scurried up the stairs, yelling, "I'll get it. You stay with our company."

"Company? More like intruders or invaders," I shot back. Then I turned my attention to my next victim. "Dillan, what's on your mind?"

Dillan shifted, uncomfortable with being put on the spot. He glanced at Lisa and back to me. What he said sent a cold spike through my chest. "The UC are *learning*. A small horde showed up while you were out bashing your head into steel doors. Our obstacles worked as planned. But only on their front line; the trailing monsters stopped short of entering the area." He paused then locked eyes with me. "Otto, they stood stock-still until we attacked them. After we killed the first UC, they moved as a team toward the wall. It's a troubling development."

"Well, Dillan. You get a gold star for being the only person here to deliver useful information. Albeit terrifying information, it is at least useful." I chewed on the news before continuing, "Did it appear that they might figure out how to defeat our defenses?"

Dillan shook his head while answering, "No, not yet. But I'm praying they don't keep learning. We're in deep trouble if they become an organized fighting unit."

That thought about killed me. We didn't stand a snowball's chance in Hell if that happened. The thought of losing to the mindless monsters running around our world infuriated me. A million thoughts fought for my brain's attention, but only one was clear. Time for some offense.

I spoke in the same order as thoughts entered my head. "Okay, we take the fight to them. It's time to up-armor the dump trucks. I'll also talk to Willis about getting a replacement for the Hummer and more gear. We'll keep them as far away from our home as possible. We'll need more volunteers. Have you installed the early warning devices? Can we move them further out? We need explosives; I'll add that to the list for Willis. Are the drones operational? We need to find fuel. Probably find some abandoned tanker trucks on the freeway ..."

I faded off when I noticed four stunned faces staring back at me. I jumped when my gear slammed to the floor and Darline spoke, "Otto, you're doing it again. Slow down, organize your thoughts, and remember that when you ask a question, you should wait for an answer. Otherwise, you're just giving orders."

"And you should remember that it's not nice to sneak up on people, Darline." Problem was she wasn't wrong.

I took a deep calming breath, made eye contact with each member of the *intervention* gang, and said, "Anything else? Tesha, what's your beef with me? I promise I'll stop teaching Devon how to swear."

She flinched when I called her out, and I realized that she'd never seen me *in action* before. I've been told it's an unpleasant experience. I think people are just soft. Nevertheless, she appeared shell-shocked, so I attempted to put her at ease and said, "I'm not crazy." It was the best I could muster under the circumstances.

"No, Otto. I have no complaints to file or concerns to voice. Actually, when I told Will about joining the team, he asked me to come with him for backup. Now I understand why. Honestly, we had no idea all this mess was happening. I'd like to go home now."

After a long gut laugh, my intervention came to an end. I saw them out and figured the issue was closed.

I attempted to shut the door, but Lisa pivoted and stuffed her foot against the door. She grabbed my collar, leaned in, and whispered, "You better nut-up, old man. We need your sorry ass." She shoved me back while releasing her grip, gave me a wink, and trotted off to catch up with Dillan.

It stunned me. Of all the people on the team, I'd figured Lisa would be happy I quit.

I turned to find that Darline had already scurried off to get ready for bed, and I decided to join her. I stood in the bathroom taking a hard look at myself in the mirror. My face and body were battered; I had twice as much gray hair as before the apocalypse started, and I looked tired. But, at that instant, my dad's voice rang in my head. It was loud and crystal clear. *Rest if you must, but don't you ever quit!*

Darline poked her head through the door and gave me a knowing smile, "What'd your dad say?" she asked.

"Whittier's poem."

"I'll wake you up in time for Tesha's training."

CHAPTER 27
ADRIFT

Shafter launched into an obscenity-laced tirade when the Tri-hull's motor sputtered to a stop. He rushed to the boat's stern and yanked open the bench seat covering the gas tank. He knew what he'd find, and he was right. The tank was empty.

With no navigational equipment on board, and only open water surrounding him, he had no idea where he was. The thought of starving to death or succumbing to exposure in the middle of Lake Erie forced another burst of obscene language from his mouth.

Shoulders slumped in resignation, Senator Shafter slid down the gunwale, slammed to the deck, and curled into a fetal position. He sobbed uncontrollably while he replayed the events that had led him to be adrift and hopeless. All the near misses and narrow escapes from the dead and angry living and this was how he met his end. Crying like a child in the middle of nowhere.

His anger surged, urging him to stand and scream, "NO! This is not how my life ends." He searched his crumbling mind for a way out, for a way to save his slimy life.

"Phone! Where is Piles' phone?" He patted his jacket, looking for his last chance to save himself. Relief flooded his system when his right hand found the girth of Piles' sat-phone in his breast pocket.

He knew who to call and what to say to save himself. He chuckled at the sweet taste of revenge filling his mouth as he thumbed on the phone. His search only took a second because the number he needed was the last number called. "Well, you sneaky hagfish, why did you call Mallet? Well, whatever the reason, he doesn't seem to have cared."

Shafter wiped sweat from his eyes with grime-covered hands, then pressed the send button. After what felt like an eternity, the call connected, and a familiar voice filled the tiny speaker. Through heavy interference, the voice spoke in a frosty tone, "I'm not sure how you lived, Piles. And I really don't care. You're worthless. Good luck surviving on your own."

"Chairman Mallet, this is Senator Shafter. Please don't hang up. I can assure you Piles is dead. I made certain it was a painful death, one she deserved."

"What do you want, Shafter? I'm fighting to save this country and enjoy precious little time for traitors."

"I know where President Wharton is hiding. I also possess the intelligence surrounding the creation of the virus."

The line went silent, causing Shafter to panic that the call had dropped. His jaw hinged open as he intended to proclaim his loyalty to Right America when Mallet spoke. "What's in it for you? I'm assuming you need your ass pulled from a king-sized jam. Talk quickly before I lose interest."

"Well, it seems you understand me better than I thought ..."

"Shafter, I told you to speak."

Stumbling over his words, Shafter finally regained his composure and said, "I'm in the middle of Lake Erie. If you want the information I have, you'll be obligated to send a rescue team for me."

Mallet's silence was deafening, but his words brought an arrogant grin to Shafter's face. "We will triangulate your position. Do not turn your phone off. If we lose the signal, we will abandon our search."

CHAPTER 28
INTRODUCTIONS

Willis' anger battled his brain for control of his mouth. He'd kept it clamped, but if this conversation continued much longer, his anger would win. The warfighter sat at the oversized conference table flanked by Chief Warrant Officer Albright to his right and First Lieutenant Billings to his left. The confident voice emanating from the conference phone belonged to Sergeant Major McMaster, out of Fort Riley. Willis had never met the man but already despised him.

"LT, I've already told you, two very important people shoved these papers into my hand and ordered me to make it happen." McMaster was responding, for the fourth time, to the same question asked four different ways.

Billings wasn't happy with the answer and was downright pissed that whoever these VIPs were didn't have the decency to deliver the news themselves.

"Tell me again, Sergeant McMaster, who issued the orders?"

"LT, this'll be the fifth time. Please listen carefully. I didn't get their names. They refused to tell me." After a pause, he continued and added some additional details, "They got off a large black motorcoach. They wore black

ACUs which held no identifying insignia. My guess is Secret Service, the ones nobody's supposed to know about."

Willis went cold at McMaster's description of the men. They sounded like the same ones guarding the Vice President. But why? What role did Willis play in this? Why transfer him to Fort Riley?

"Sergeant Major, this is Sergeant Willis. I have a question for you."

"Please, for God's sake, don't ask the same question a sixth time."

"Understood, Sir. This bus, does it house a large television on its passenger side?"

"Affirmative. Why?"

Wills screwed his eyes shut. He realized he wouldn't be able to wiggle out of the assignment because it came from Vice President Pace. He responded to the man who would soon be his CO, "Thank you, Sir. I now have a clear understanding of the situation. I'll report to Riley in forty-eight hours."

"McMaster, this is Lieutenant Billings. Inform your CO and whoever else needs to know, I'm releasing Sergeant Willis under protest. Camp Hopkins is in no position to lose troops, especially ones of Willis' caliber! I assure you, this is only a temporary assignment."

"Understood, Sir. Willis, find me upon your arrival."

Billings disconnected the call before Willis could reply to McMaster, his anger on full display. He glared at Albright and asked, "What are our options?"

Albright took a deep breath and glanced at Willis. "That depends on who requested the transfer. Willis, I noticed your reaction when McMaster answered your question. What did his answer mean to you?"

Willis leaned back in his chair and fixed Albright in a hard stare. "The men that gave McMaster the transfer paperwork belong to Vice President Pace's security detail. It appears the orders are coming from the VP." Pausing, Willis glanced at both men and said, "I need to tell my family. I request to depart Hopkins immediately and get my affairs in order."

"Request granted. And Willis, you will return to Hopkins double-quick. Dismissed," Billings said.

Willis stormed down the hallway leading to his locker. His intent was to empty it, talk to his men, and bug out ASAP. He had much to accomplish and couldn't afford to waste a second of his time.

The events of the day tumbled around his head as he marched through the busy military installation. His thoughts broken when Albright called to him, he snapped around to find his CO jogging after him.

"Willis, are you heading to the community?"

"That's my intent. After I clear out my locker and talk to my squad, I'll be spending time with my family."

"Good. I'd like you to introduce your temporary replacement to them. Master Sergeant Lucas, from Entry Point One, just arrived. Hold tight while I round her up."

"I'm sorry, Sir, can you repeat that?"

Albright shot Willis a puzzled look and answered, "Master Sergeant Lucas, from Entry Point One. Something I need to know, Willis?"

Willis, his amusement with the situation boiling over, said, "That's what I thought. Nothing to worry about, Sir. But I can't wait to see Otto's face when he meets my replacement. At least something good came from this." He spun on his heel and headed off to gather his belongings and talk to his team.

Thirty minutes later, Willis pulled to the main gate of the community, with MS Lucas following in a separate Humvee. He was happy that his family now called this place home. His younger brother and sister had quickly taken to their new surroundings. Considering that Logan was nineteen and Addie had recently turned eighteen, Willis had worried about the transition. But both embraced the opportunity to contribute and become part of something as close to normal as one can achieve in today's world.

It surprised Willis when Andy greeted them at the gate. Otto told him that Andy had been released from quarantine, but he was unaware that he had been assigned to a security detail.

"Hey, Sergeant Willis, good to see you. Who's that tagging along?" Andy said while bobbing his head in Lucas' direction.

"Oh, she's an old friend of Otto's. I'm reintroducing them today. Is the one-man wrecking-crew around?"

"He's training with the team. Actually, from the chatter on the radio, he's supervising and giving direction more than training."

Willis chuckled at Andy's choice of words and quickly corrected him. "You mean he's being a pain in the ass, again."

It was Andy's turn to laugh. "That, Sergeant Willis, is the truth. We'll get you through bite inspection and send you on your way. You're in for a treat; your brother's manning the inspection tent."

Willis' eyes clouded at the mention of his brother. Andy noticed Willis' reaction and asked, "Everything okay? He's doing a good job. So is your sister. They fit right in and neither of them is afraid of getting their hands dirty."

Willis broke his thought and said, "I'm good, I just need to talk to them about something. Let's get a move on. Oh, and Andy. How are you feeling? You look damn healthy."

Andy's smile stretched the width of his face, and he said, "I feel damn healthy, thanks for asking."

Their conversation was interrupted by a gruff voice emanating from the second Humvee. "Are you two going to kiss? I can leave and give you some privacy."

Willis put his hand up, signaling Lucas to calm down, and looked at Andy. "If you can break away from guard duty, you'll want to come see Otto's reaction when he sees her."

Andy, still gawking at Lucas' Humvee, said, "From the scowl on her face, I'd say Otto's in trouble."

"Andy, you don't know the half of it."

CHAPTER 29
FORT RILEY

Sergeant Major McMaster marched towards the temporary housing units occupying the Mounted Color Guard Demo Area bordering the Kansas River. He loved this part of Riley; the wooded area and river had always calmed him. Now, the picturesque setting was a stain on the home of The Big Red One, an overcrowded, filthy mess of Blue States United whiners incapable of even picking up their own trash. It appeared they felt basic sanitation was someone else's responsibility.

In addition to the call with Camp Hopkins, McMaster had received a letter from his CO. The missive pushed him past his breaking point. It was a "Formal Demand" submitted by a group calling themselves "The Voice of BSU Survivors of the Massacre Perpetrated by RAM"—henceforth to be referred to as "The Survivors." *They really love forming committees*, he thought as his rising anger quickened his pace. The letter prompted him to relieve Corporal Dunn of his morning duties of corralling the refugees to the makeshift mess hall, two hundred yards from their temporary housing.

The Survivors demanded that the base housing be divided between them and the current residents. That thought made his teeth grind. *You want to displace warfighters and their families. The same fighters that plucked your worthless hides from a country YOUR government, not RAM, allowed to be overrun.*

He reached the section of the "Formal Demand" that had initially set him off. *In addition to accommodation equity, we declare our encampment a gun-free zone. Your instruments of death and control are not welcome where BSU refugees reside.*

The Survivors hereby demand more diverse meal options. Ones that accurately represent the multicultural community of The Survivors being forcibly detained by our oppressors at Fort Riley. Furthermore, our constant exposure to the cultural appropriation perpetrated by your meal preparers has become a triggering event for many of The Survivors. Please discontinue the use of the following terms: Chinese food (Orange Chicken, Sweet and Sour Chicken, and Kung Pao Chicken). Mexican food (Tacos, Burritos, and Refried Beans). We trust you are now clear on our meaning and will act with haste to rectify this deficiency. The Survivors also look forward to the addition of options for vegans, vegetarians, the lactose intolerant, and gluten intolerant.

With thirty years of service behind him, the six-foot-two-inch, powerfully built McMaster had served his country in many roles. His favorite was his time as Drill Sergeant McMaster. Shaping young, soft men into warfighters was his greatest accomplishment. A smile went crooked on his face as he left Marshall Avenue and approached the first of the large olive-drab tents serving as housing for the BSU refugees. The smile widened because today he would relive his days as a drill sergeant.

McMaster barked into the megaphone, "Breakfast is served. Get your ass off your cot, get dressed, and fall in line."

He moved sharply through the housing, barking the message into each tent. The peevish inhabitants stirred in their cots. A chorus of discontent rose to a crescendo as insults were spit in his direction. Now he understood why Dunn was happy to be relieved of this assignment.

"I find your insults triggering. I do not respond well when I am triggered. Now shut up, form up, and let the RAM Military provide you with some healthy nourishment."

The wide-eyed and confused faces of the refugees, now silent, stared back at him.

"Well done. I have hope for you yet. Line up single file, NOW!"

He really had missed his bullhorn. The sound of his angry voice, mixed with a hint of violence, was music to his ears.

McMasters walked the line of refugees, looking for the signs that would identify the writers of the "Formal Demand." He found them more quickly than expected. A group of six—four men and two women—walked deliberately slow to join the line. Each displayed bravado that would last only as long as he stood thirty yards away.

He stormed in their direction while his voice blasted through his bullhorn, "Nice of you to join us. Because you held up breakfast for the others, you will move to the back of the line." He now stood mere inches from the group as they cowered from the deafening message and covered their ears. "As a reward for your behavior, we will all take an extended tour of the grounds before breakfast. MOVE OUT."

Groans of displeasure raced along the line.

"What's that you say? You'd like to walk even further before breakfast. Well, I am surprised. You may not be the lazy, privileged slugs I thought you were."

"Excuse me, Sir. Where is the soldier who usually escorts us to breakfast?" a mousy young man asked.

McMaster almost burst out laughing; *this one doesn't understand how it works.*

Bullhorn touching Mousy Man's nose, McMaster answered as a drill sergeant should. "Young man, thank you for volunteering the group for an additional one-hundred-yard hike this fine morning."

Mousy Man attempted to slink away from the deafening voice, but McMaster moved with him.

"Corporal Dunn had complained of *triggering* behavior from this group." He snapped his head to the left to watch the reaction of the gang of six. As he'd expected, he received squinty-eyed glares accompanied by tough-guy posturing. *The guilty are so predictable.*

"I'll pass your concern on. It'll make him all aflutter knowing how much you all miss him. Now, we need to accomplish a lot of walking before breakfast. Move!"

McMaster took the group of two hundred on a mile-long hike while reciting the history of Fort Riley and the brave men and women who called it home. As he walked the line shouting commands at the refugees, he paid special attention to the six people at the back of the line. Their sweaty faces straining to keep up warmed his soul. The surprise waiting for them at the end of the hike made him downright giddy.

When they reached the mess hall, he stopped them at the entrance. "Well done, ladies and gentlemen. Tomorrow, we work on cutting the time it took for the hike by a full twenty-five percent. You may now eat your breakfast."

He pushed the entrance flap open and allowed them to enter. The gasps and grumbled confusion of the group when empty chafing pans greeted them was immensely satisfying.

Feigning shock, McMaster began ranting, "What happened? Why isn't your breakfast awaiting your arrival?" He continued with his eyes wide in mock-disbelief, "Did the cooks quit? Maybe something triggered them?" Placing his left index finger on his lower lip, he gazed at the ceiling as if pondering the meaning of life. "I wonder what it could be?" He shoved his finger skyward and exclaimed, "I've got it! People who won't clean up their own filth triggered them. People who complained about the food RAM feeds them triggered them. Ignorant, lazy people who don't contribute to Fort Riley's success triggered them."

His voice blared through his trusty bullhorn as he finished, "Today, you become productive members of this facility. If you choose not to participate, we won't feed you. If you do not eat, you will die, because Fort Riley lacks the resources to care for dumbasses!"

As he stared back at the stunned faces fixated on his every word, he brought the bullhorn to bear on their senses one last time. "You will return to your housing and clean it; you will then report back here and form a line at the green tents being erected outside the mess hall. You will be given work assignments by the soldiers manning those green tents. After receiving your assignment, you may eat."

McMaster walked to the back of the line and barked, "You six remain here. The rest of you are dismissed."

The crowd scattered like rats, rushing to obey McMaster's orders. *Hunger's got a way to tame a man's pride.* His father's quote forced a chuckle at the refugee's expense.

When the mess hall grew still, he fixed the gang of six with a hard stare and removed his drill sergeant hat. He addressed them in a low growl. "With six of you, this might be a fair fight."

Chapter 30
Endless Sacrifices

From my perch atop Jackson's truck, I informed the team how thoroughly disappointed I was. It wasn't even noon, and they were already winded. Crying around about the heat, extra calisthenics, heavy packs. Bunch of crybabies!

The only bright spot had been Tesha's knowledge of our weapons. Moreover, her ability to use them proved awe-inspiring. We'd planned to start the day by familiarizing her with our arsenal. However, she quickly grew tired of my lecture and grabbed an M4 and field-stripped it in under a minute. While I stared at her, slack-jawed, she re-assembled it just as quickly and shoved it at me for inspection, so I did. It was perfect.

She moved to the SAW (Squad Automatic Weapon) and repeated the process. It took a bit longer, but she still moved through the process with lightning speed. I was impressed, mostly because I had no idea how to strip the SAW. But what she did next blew us away.

She fed a belt of 5.56 ammo onto the feed tray, slammed the cover, pulled the charging handle, and yelled, "Range is hot." This was immediately followed by the sensual sound of hundreds of rounds being hurled downrange and obliterating our targets, one hundred yards away.

When the last metallic belt link clanged off the pavement, Tesha continued staring downrange, admiring her handiwork, and said, "It's been a while. I'm a little rusty. Can we get to work now?"

And that marked the end of me being impressed with the team. From that point on, they just disappointed me. I would have demonstrated how to perform their training drills, but I was still concussed and following my doctor's orders to take it easy. However, even in my wounded condition, I was still able to impart my wisdom. Plus all the *coaching* I was doing was making my head hurt ... the sacrifices I made for this team were endless.

The team had nearly finished running the last of the five additional laps I'd assigned them when Lisa locked eyes with me and mouthed, *I'm going to kill you.*

Her threat was the final straw. "Real nice, Lisa. I'm putting my heart and soul into making you the perfect fighting machine. I'm here, sacrificing my body yet again, when I should be at home convalescing. And you show your gratitude by threatening to kill me? Unbelievable!"

The team finished their run about the same time I finished my rant. They stumbled to the finish line, dripping with sweat and gasping for air. Stone fell to the ground and began kneading a painful cramp in his right calf. He fixed me in a hard stare and growled, "Otto, if I get my hands on you in the next five minutes, I will kill you. No threats, I'll actually kill you!"

"That's it, I'm done here," I screamed. "I'm leaving. I need to return Jack's truck and tend to some important business. You can all kiss my royal-red-ass, you ungrateful SOBs."

Thirty seconds later, I raced away from the training area, but I didn't head to Jackson's house. I had an important stop to make.

Stone glanced at Tesha and asked, "It's time for his walk with Devon, isn't it?"

She checked the time and smiled. "It is. Your brother's a good man. Unbalanced, and possibly suffering from some developmental challenges, but a good man nonetheless."

Stone laughed. "He has his moments. But mostly, he's a pain-in-the-ass."

He was stunned when Lisa chimed in, "Yeah, but he's *our* pain-in-the-ass."

Her statement also surprised Will. "Lisa, are you feeling okay?"

Caught off guard and clearly embarrassed that she said something endearing about Otto, she hardened her features and, in her patented gregarious style, said, "WHAT? He's our pain-in-the-ass because we're stuck with the oaf." Greeted by doubting smiles, Lisa barked, "BACK TO WORK. Let's practice clearing some houses!"

Chapter 31
One Percent

Doctor McCune pored over their charts even as the full-auto gunfire erupted around him. *What happened? What caused the violent reaction in these particular subjects?*

"Doctor, let's go. NOW!" Sims barked at him. The soldier's tone made it clear that his patience had run out.

A frantic McCune responded, "I need to review the charts. I need to understand why this happened."

The soldier stood between the entrance to the main room of the mobile hospital and McCune's small office area. He was yelling at McCune over his shoulder, imploring the man to evacuate. But McCune had a laser focus on the medical charts on his desk.

Sims' M4 rattled to life a moment later, tearing through a creature blocked from the doctor's sight, but not from his ears. Its deafening screech sent a terrified McCune into action.

"Well, I suppose I can just bring the charts with me," he said as he rushed to secure the data and get to safety.

Sims brought his M4 online once again. The soldier's weapon unleashed a seemingly endless string of death upon the monsters wreaking havoc in the mobile hospital.

McCune slammed to a stop when Sims again stepped back, further into the tight area.

"Doctor, is there another exit we can use? They've blocked the main aisle."

McCune considered the layout of the facility. Its steel framework prevented them from cutting through the heavy canvas serving as the unit's skin. They were quickly losing ground to the savages. McCune instinctively stepped back as Sims retreated further into the room. The idea struck the doctor as his left foot landed on the section of loose flooring he had been meaning to have replaced. The facility's floor was raised two feet off the ground. Their exit had just revealed itself.

"The floor, Mister Sims! We can exit through the floor!" he yelled while bending down and trying to wrench the loose plywood up. It wouldn't budge. It was positioned too tightly next to the other sections of flooring which made it impossible to secure a grip and pry it away from its support beams.

Sims dared a glance over his shoulder and immediately recognized the situation. He turned back to the advancing enemy and emptied his magazine into their ranks. Then he retreated to the doctor's position, removed his K-BAR 1213, forced it into the space between the sections of flooring, and pried the piece up.

He gripped the plywood, yanked it free, and screamed at McCune to move. Not waiting to see if the doctor followed his command, he turned and heaved the plywood at the entrance to the office. The rough slab of wood slammed into the throat of the leading monster, knocking it to the floor.

Down to his sidearm, Sims un-holstered the Sig-M17. Its extended magazine held twenty-one 9mm FMJ rounds. The beast had regained its footing and stood motionless, staring at him as if contemplating its next move. Sims was awestruck by two things. It seemed to be strategizing, and it didn't appear to be a UC. Instead, a spider web of dark veins covered its body, bulging through virtually translucent skin.

Sims snapped from his stupor and sent three rounds through the fiend's head. His shots were rapidly followed by full-auto gunfire coming from within the mobile hospital. "It's about damn time you guys showed up!" he shouted over the racket created by the battle waging a few feet from his position. He pivoted to join McCune, relieved to find the doctor had already made his escape.

Sims entered the hole in the floor headfirst and began leopard-crawling to safety when suddenly his left leg stopped dead. Instinct told him what was happening; he wasn't tangled in the floor's support beams. He was in the grasp of one of the monsters the antidote had created.

A flash later, he was being dragged backward with a force beyond his comprehension. His head slammed against the edge of the floorboards as he exited the hole. The vicious blow sent him spiraling toward unconsciousness. Dark clouds filled his vision but not quickly enough to spare him from witnessing his captor's wicked grin as it prepared to strike.

McCune kicked the corrugated metal skirt covering the mobile hospital's raised foundation and shimmied into the blinding daylight. His lab coat, now streaked with grass and mud, flapped open when he spun to peer through the hole for Sims. Dread consumed him when he found nothing but a black void.

"Soldier, where are you? If you're lost, follow my voice." Tears stung his eyes as reality took hold. His voice shattering, he shouted, "Young man, please answer me … please!" He paused, straining to hear the brave young man's reply, but it never came.

McCune fell to his knees and screamed, "I'm sorry, I'm so very sorry."

Hope jolted his eyes open when he heard something large hit the ground, followed by the scuffling sound of someone crawling just out of sight. "Follow my voice! Just a few more feet and you'll be safe."

When he received no response, he asked, "Are you injured? I'm coming to help." The doctor got on hands and knees and began to crawl into the hole and towards the void. He recoiled as something heavy bounced into view. His mind twisted as the soldier's crudely severed head rolled to a stop inches from his left hand and locked eyes with him.

McCune screamed as the severed head's mouth hinged open, allowing its tongue to loll onto its battered cheek. He lurched backward then struggled to his feet, trying to escape the ghastly scene. He hurriedly bent to collect his notes and caught movement from the corner of his eye. Turning his head, he came face to face with a blood-stained monster.

Frozen in fear, he braced for death to take him. Suddenly, he heard a deafening blast and the beast's head snapped to the side, blood bursting from its skull. Covered in brain matter and gore, McCune was suddenly being dragged away from the opening, then deposited roughly on the ground.

Within seconds, the area was swarming with heavily armed troops. A huge soldier known to McCune as Sergeant Timmons barked orders to the men and women converging on the scene. After a cautious moment, the sergeant gave the command to secure the motionless beast. A flurry of activity followed. Before the doctor's brain could rationalize the situation, they had secured the creature with zip-cuffs and dragged it from the opening.

McCune struggled to his feet and rushed to the side of the immobilized corpse. He began inspecting its remains. Aside from dark veins covered by nearly transparent skin, the test subject appeared completely human. It was void of the signature characteristics found on the UCs he had examined. And it remained warm to his touch.

Something else was missing. "Sergeant, did the subjects experiencing the reaction attempt to consume their victims?"

A furious Sergeant Timmons growled his response. "Negative. They appeared to slaughter my soldiers for sport." He paused a moment and then launched a string of accusation-tinged questions, "What fresh Hell have you unleashed on us? Why didn't you order the test subjects to be restrained? Can we expect the others you injected to react the same way?"

McCune tuned the sergeant out after he confirmed his suspicions. The lack of a blood-soaked mouth showed the subject was not interested in feeding; only killing.

McCune interrupted Timmons. "Sergeant, I'm unable to answer your questions. But it is imperative that you deliver this subject to my lab immediately!"

Twenty minutes later, McCune sat dumbfounded at his desk. He and Doctor Kris had quickly discovered the link between the subjects experiencing the reaction.

"All subjects had AB negative blood types, all of them," Kris repeated. "Our human trial test group had a disproportionally high number of AB negative samples."

"Then we should expect one percent of all living beings to experience the same violent reaction displayed by the subjects, after the antidote is metabolized." The antidote was designed to be absorbed through the eyes and skin of the UC, increasing, tenfold, the rate at which the antidote reached the brain. The revelation promised to crush McCune.

"Doctor Kris, what are the blood types of the UCs we have tested? More importantly, are any of the subjects AB negative?"

With the same horrifying thought as Doctor McCune, Doctor Kris had already pulled the test charts up on her laptop.

"No, none of the original test subjects have type AB negative blood." Eyes wide with fear, she faced McCune and said, "It's imperative that we find UC subjects with the blood type. Can we suspend production?"

McCune studied the charts and had a terrifying epiphany. Blood type dictated the level of mutation the UCs achieved. He immediately grabbed his encrypted phone and hit the send button. *We must stop production of the antidote.*

After one ring, his call was answered. "I assume you're calling with good news about the human trial, Doctor."

"No, in fact, I'm not. You must supply me with a level two UC, and we must halt antidote production. The antidote had a violent reaction in a sub-segment of the test subjects. We need to understand why."

After a long silence, the voice spoke, "Impossible. We've already added the blue dye to the antidote, our Global Hawk UAVs are preparing for recon flights, F22s are en route to destroy the bridges as we speak, and we've retrofitted the C130s for the drop. We intend to move forward in forty-eight hours."

The chosen test area was the island city of Alameda, California. Its location enabled the military to demolish the access bridges, isolating the city's seventy-five thousand residents for observation after administering the antidote. The intent of adding blue dye was to identify which UC received the aerosolized treatment. It would allow for drone reconnaissance of the area and then help identify subjects to extract for study at McCune's lab.

McCune exploded when his request was denied; he shot to his feet and screamed, "Do you understand the implications of your actions? You may eliminate all human life from the planet if you move forward."

Greeted by silence, McCune checked the phone's display and found the call had been disconnected.

CHAPTER 32
ON TIME

I checked my watch and determined I'd be on time, but only if I threw caution to the wind and avoided running over anyone unfortunate enough to wander into my path. I figured since I was driving Jackson's truck, he'd get blamed for my recklessness. So I stomped the gas pedal to the floorboard, causing the oversized truck to careen through the streets of our community.

I probably should've been more careful, but I had somewhere important to be. And I needed to arrive there before Randy. It was as simple as that.

The truck power-slid around the last corner and rocketed down the pin-straight street. My destination was in sight, and Randy was nowhere to be seen. Then it happened: Pat stepped directly into my path and threw her hand up in a *stop the damn truck* motion.

I stood on the brake pedal and cut the wheel hard to the left. A cold sweat covered my body while the truck fought against my choice and continued on a beeline in Pat's direction.

She didn't even flinch when the now *slightly* out-of-control truck bounced off the curb, shot hard to the right, and screeched to halt, touching her outstretched hand. The woman never ceases to amaze and frankly, scare the shit out of me.

She held me in a withering glare while marching from the front of Jackson's truck to my closed window. Not a chance I would roll down the window, inviting her wrath into the truck. Instead, I smiled and yelled from the safety of the sealed cab, "Whew, thanks for doing that, Pat. I got distracted and lost track of my speed. Hell, I could have killed someone if not for your brave actions." I followed up with my best toothy grin.

It fell as flat as I figured it would, and my fear grew at the same speed her face reddened with anger. "Otto Hammer, if you were my son, we wouldn't be having this conversation. Do you know why?" I shook my head slowly while keeping an eye on her hands, in case she decided to punch through the window and wring my neck. She continued, "Well, I would have donated you to the circus shortly after you learned to speak. Because at that point, I would have determined something was terribly wrong with you."

"Wow, that was mean, Pat. I think I'll just go now. I can see I'm not appreciated here." I stealthily slipped the truck into gear, simultaneously prompting Pat to act..

She slapped the window and shouted at me to stop. I did. Like I said, she's scary.

I powered down the window, and Pat pinned my ears back. "What in the name of ... are you crazy? What on earth possessed you to drive this metal killing machine through our neighborhood like you're racing in the Indy 500?"

I opened my mouth to explain, but Pat continued her rant, "Never mind, I don't want to hear your stupid excuse. That's not the reason I want to talk to you, anyway. Now that you seem fully recovered from being *concussed*, as you call it, we need to call a meeting. Fall is around the corner, and there are a ton of issues to address if we plan to survive through winter. Be at my house tonight at five o'clock."

"Um, Pat. Can I go now? I promise to be at the meeting."

"Oh, just get out of my face. But do it slowly this time!"

I pulled away, keeping an eye on her hands until I cleared her punching zone. When I set my eyes back on the road, Randy's hulking frame came into view. My foot instinctively pushed the gas pedal to the floor, rocketing the F250 in his direction.

I powered down the passenger window and yelled as I sped past him, "Not today, my bearded friend."

Randy gave me a quizzical look. Probably because he didn't realize this was a competition, and I wasn't going to explain it to him.

I skidded to a stop in front of Tesha's house and scrambled from the truck. Devon was waiting on the porch with his aunt. I think her name is May.

His smile was infectious as he shouted, "Mister Otto. You were almost late. I was going to start our inspections without you."

Randy lumbered up a moment later and received the same greeting. He was winded, and a bead of sweat trickled from his hairline. I glanced over at him and said, "You tried to beat me, didn't you? Sure ya did. You figured it out and ran like the wind, a slow lumbering and ugly wind, to beat me here. Silly Randy."

I believe that if his arm wasn't immobilized, he would have punched me. His eyes bugged, joining his flared nostrils, and he said, "*Mister* Otto, please be quiet."

Our exchange elicited a laugh from Devon and his aunt. Then the little man pulled his notebook out and proclaimed, "I made notes and plans. We gotta whip these people into shape!"

I glanced down at Devon and said, "Yes we do, Sir. Yes, we do. First, I need to talk to you. Can you ask Mister Randy to give us some privacy?"

Devon's face screwed up with confusion, but he soldiered on. "Mister Randy, what Otto said!"

Randy couldn't help himself and burst out laughing. "Well, Mister Devon. I can acquiesce to your request." This garnered more confused looks from Devon and his aunt.

Devon and I walked a few feet away, and I said, "Hey, little man. I wanted to tell you that I may miss some of our inspections over the next few weeks. I'm feeling better, and

I'll be training with your mom. But I promise you, I'll stop by to say hello as often as I can. And when I do, we can review your notes and develop a plan to get things back on track."

Devon stared through me for a long minute. He motioned for me to get closer to him so I bent over with my hands on my knees. Devon went to his tiptoes and whispered, "Promise me you'll keep my mom safe."

The weight of his innocent request tightened my chest. I tried to speak, but the words caught in my throat. So I nodded and offered a pinky-swear, and I meant it.

CHAPTER 33
I DIDN'T

As the skinny man soared, screaming, past her head, the woman dressed in black asked, "You wouldn't hit a woman, would you?"

Her cowering posture didn't fool McMaster. He grinned and said, "No, ma'am, never have, nor will I ever strike a woman." As expected, the anarchist paid no attention to her comrade, crumpled at her feet, and attacked. Claw-like neon green nails led her charge while she screeched her intention to gouge out McMaster's eyes.

McMaster shifted his head left, then, in one fluid motion, placed his right hand on her throat, hooked his right leg behind hers, and slammed her to the ground. The woman's head bounced off the hard-packed earth serving as the mess hall floor.

While on one knee next to the dazed woman, her accomplices seized the opportunity and attacked McMaster.

McMaster lifted the delirious woman by her filthy shirt and thick, spike-covered belt and tossed her at his assailant's legs. Her skeleton-thin body sent three ungrateful thugs to the ground in a tangled heap.

On his feet in a flash, he squared up with the last remaining attacker. Hatred filled the eyes of the man closing on McMaster from six feet away. A flash later, McMaster was holding the doughy man-child by his neck. The stunned punk thrashed and pulled at McMaster's hand, struggling to breathe.

A moment before the man fell unconscious, McMaster flung him at his friends as they struggled to stand, once again slamming them all to the ground.

"You need to understand something. The moment you attacked me, you became enemy combatants. RAM is no longer taking prisoners. That means I'm duty-bound to execute you right here, right now."

The sergeant major approached the group of agitators still on the ground and asked, "Do you want to become useful citizens of Fort Riley? Or would you rather be delivered back to your precious Blue States United?" He waited for an answer as the thugs struggled to their feet. When no answer came, he screamed, "Answer my question!"

The group exchanged nervous glances before sheepishly answering that they wanted to stay at Fort Riley.

Sergeant Major McMaster nodded as he glared at the demoralized group. "That's what I thought. Do you have questions before you get in line for your work assignments?"

The woman he had slammed to the ground found one last thing to gripe about. "Why should we trust you? How do we know you won't whisk us away in the middle of the night and send us back to BSU?"

Annoyed by the insult to his integrity, he barked his answer, "Because I gave you my word."

The woman pressed her challenge, and her luck, when she countered him, "You also told me you wouldn't hit a woman."

McMaster smiled and said, "I didn't hit you."

The woman's face flushed at the revelation, and she answered, "That's an accurate statement, Sergeant Major."

"I'm happy you agree. Now, get in line and know that I'll be watching you. Oh, and here's your letter," he said, throwing the folded paper at them. "Maybe you can use it to draw some hearts and unicorns to decorate your bunks."

With that, McMaster about-faced and exited the tent.

As he inspected the refugees waiting for work assignments, four Black Hawk helicopters thundered overhead. The sight puzzled him; nothing in the morning briefing had mentioned activity that required the big beautiful warbirds to take flight.

Curiosity winning out, he barked a question at Private Beck standing guard at the work detail tents. "Why are we airborne today, Beck?"

Beck responded with haste. "Intel received from the Joint Chiefs. They discovered a breach in the wall, Sir."

The news sent anxiety through the refugees and caused McMaster to bolt towards the Tactical Operation Center.

He yelled one last question to Beck. "Scope of the breach?"

Beck's response was unsettling. "Unknown."

CHAPTER 34
BRIGADE

"I am your leader. My name is Bobby Smith. You have enlisted in the most fearsome army to have ever walked the earth. You will wreak havoc upon our enemies. We will show no mercy, spare no life. Today you join the ranks of the soldiers already marching towards victory!"

Bobby paced frantically in front of his troops, his ears registering their thunderous reply of solidarity. His excitement grew as he envisioned his army crushing his enemy! This outpost, the one he had been monitoring for almost a week, must fall. It must fall in grand fashion. It would send a message to all the survivors that they would never be safe. *That I can strike at any moment with devastating power!*

He stepped closer to his men, the stench of their collective bodies overpowering his senses. But he pushed on. "When our forces unite, we will reach full brigade strength. Our numbers will be such that their walls will crumble under our boots!"

He raised his arms in victory and awaited the cheers of his eager warriors. The sound stinging his ears was not that of combat-ready warriors. It was the raspy drone of the undead.

Reality spun into focus like a whirlpool, sucking his glorious vision to the sea's darkest depths. His world tilted at the sight, his thoughts tumbling so violently he went off balance. He reached his hand out and grabbed a metal pole supporting the remnants of a child's swing set. Pulling himself close to the cool metal, Bobby wrapped his arms around the pole as tightly as possible.

Tears streamed from his eyes as he begged, "Not now, please not now! YOU'VE taken everything from me. Please don't take my mind!"

"You're pathetic! Look at you, sniveling like a snot-nosed baby. What's wrong, little baby, did you shit your pants again? Huh, that's why the bitch left you in a trashcan, isn't it? You smelled so vile your own mother couldn't bear the shame you brought her!"

Still clinging to the pole, Bobby tried to strip the thoughts from his mind, but their thorns held fast. Herbert was right. Bobby Smith was a broken, pathetic, empty husk.

"You're a bottom feeder pretending to be a noble soldier, a leader of men. You make me sick!"

Struggling to stay on his feet, Bobby willed his voice from his panic-stricken throat, "Silence!" Anger set his damaged brain aflame.

His mind began coming back online. A feeling of invincibility swept over him. Peeling away from his support, he pivoted to face his army and proclaimed, "Our time is NOW!"

He stormed to the first container and threw its heavy doors open. Then ran to the next one, and the one after that, until all fifteen containers housing his army were releasing his soldiers onto the battlefield.

He positioned himself twenty feet from the dead, waving his arms and screaming, "Are you hungry? Do you long for the sweet taste of our enemy's flesh? I will lead you to them; lead you to the thing you most desire."

Bobby kept a watchful eye on his army while slowly backing away from them. Their singular focus on consuming the living drove them to stalk his every move. Once the current of dead was strong enough to sustain itself, he screamed, "Onwards to victory!"

Bobby Smith pivoted and ran through the abandoned neighborhoods of a dying world until he reached the house he used as his camp. He bolted the door behind him and rushed to the second-level window where his sniper's nest awaited him.

After sliding behind his Dragunov, he peered through its Night Force 5.5-22x56 NXS scope and found the old man speaking with his young friend. He rested the scope's crosshairs on the child's head and whispered, "I should kill you right in front of the old man."

Indecision gripped him. Watching the old man's reaction after the child's head disappeared might be worth launching his attack now.

His finger entered the trigger guard when suddenly the pair reacted to something unseen. Panning his scope to the west brought two Humvees into focus.

Bobby pulled away from the scope and let the breath he was holding escape his lungs. It was better this way; he needed to allow his forces to engage the enemy.

A smile twisting his features, he whispered, "Soon."

Chapter 35
Old Friend

My moment with Devon broke when a pair of Hummers rumbled in our direction. I was concerned that two of them were inside our walls. Thinking the worst, I told Devon to head back inside and I called Randy over.

"Why two Hummers, Randy? This isn't a good sign."

"I agree. Feels like a shit-storm headed our way."

We both relaxed a little when Willis' gigantic head came into view, filling up the windshield of the lead Hummer. This shifted the mystery to the trailing Hummer.

Willis parked a few houses away, putting him in front of my home. He signaled for us to join him.

While we walked, I said, "I don't like it, Randy. This isn't a social visit. Something's wrong."

I looked a question at Randy when he didn't respond. He had already placed his functioning hand on his HK VP9's grip. Yep, he sensed it too. Something evil hung in the air, and it was about to blow through our home. The feeling was strong enough for me to parrot Randy's action and place my hand on my XDm.

About five feet from Willis' Hummer, we stopped. Willis shot us a puzzled look before exiting. He signaled to the second Hummer's occupant to hold. Then he asked,

"Why the hostile posture, gents? We're still on the same team."

"What's the scoop?" I asked while bobbing my head towards the other Hummer.

"Oh, that. Well, Otto, I have a surprise for you. An old friend wanted to reconnect with one of her favorite people. She said that she … oh Hell, let's just get to it."

Willis seemed far too pleased with himself. He was setting me up. I could smell it. He spun and signaled for our unknown guest to join us. With my sightline blocked by the first Hummer and Willis' giant grinning mug, my nerves went on edge. I kept my hand on my weapon and watched the unknown guest stalk into view.

Displaying a wicked grin that reached her horribly bloodshot eyes, Master Sergeant Lucas said, "Hellooo, Otto, good to see you again."

Randy burst into laughter at the same instant I nearly succumbed to shock. My mind told me to run, but my feet stayed rooted in place. Why was she sullying my home with her nasty self?

I broke out of my thoughts and asked, "Why is she here? Willis, why is this person standing here?"

My questions forced another round of laughter from Randy. My head was spinning. The second meanest person in the world stood ten feet from me. And I didn't know why.

Willis, suppressing his own laughter, said, "Well, Otto. I have some news. And honestly, your reaction is the only part I'm enjoying."

He nodded at Lucas and said, "Master Sergeant Lucas is assuming command of my squad. I'm being temporarily reassigned to Fort Riley. I ship out in forty-eight hours."

My mouth tried to catch up to my brain and moved like a gasping fish. I had several million questions for Willis and an equal number of insults for Lucas. I pulled myself together long enough to spurt out, "Well, tell Master Sergeant Lucas that our community's supply of Visine is off limits."

Willis and Lucas joined Randy, attempting to laugh me into humiliation. Oh, not today, my nasty friends. "So, you're leaving us in the hands of this wretched person? I'm surprised."

Sobering up, Lucas asked, "Surprised about what? A woman taking charge?"

"Well, that's just a stupid question. Actually, I'm surprised that the soldiers guarding Entry Point One didn't feed you to the UCs."

I swear, at that moment, birds ceased their chirping, dogs stopped barking, and children froze in place. The realization that I may have gone too far struck me at the same instant Lucas' gloved fist zipped past my head. Not just any glove, a combat glove with hard plastic knuckles molded into them. Had I not juked to the left, she would have broken my jaw.

I avoided being punched, but the move sent me off balance, and I stumbled into Randy. Bent over from laughter, he wasn't prepared when I plowed into his wounded shoulder. His roaring laughter turned to roars of pain in an instant. He spun to protect his shoulder and instead threw himself off balance. With gravity in full control, we tumbled to the street in a tangled heap of arms and legs. Unable to free my hands to break my fall, my forehead smacked the pavement, opening a small cut that bled profusely.

Willis moved to restrain the red-eyed maniac as Randy and I struggled to free ourselves from our human knot. I could hear Lucas ranting on and on about separating my head from its neck and stomping the life from my body. You know, the usual ranting from people who know me. But her threats lacked the creativity needed for me to take her seriously. I mean, I've been threatened with more flair by blue-hairs at a Vegas buffet. So I rolled to my back, lifted my bloody head, and said, "Blah, blah, blah. Come at me harder than that. Hell, my grandmother's more intimidating."

"Otto, shut up," Willis yelled while trying to calm Lucas and keep her from acting on her schoolyard-level threats.

Lucas finally struggled free of Willis' grasp and took a step in my direction. But something happened when she took in my situation. It started with a grin, morphed into a chuckle, and ended in a full-blown snorting laugh.

The tension left Willis' body when she turned to him and said, "You were right. Something about him makes you want to kill him and laugh at him at the same time. He's like, I don't know? Like a, like a …"

Willis finished Lucas' thought, "Child. A big, emotionally challenged child."

Lucas snapped her fingers and said, "You nailed it, a child!"

Randy, despite his pain, joined in. "Lisa thinks he was dropped on his head as a baby. A theory we all agree with."

Thunderous laughter followed his statement, so I just lowered my head back to the pavement and let them have their juvenile moment. Plus, my head hurt. While I stared at the beautiful sky, I realized that something seemed familiar about Lucas. Then it hit me. She was Lisa's clone, equally mean as the original, and trained to kill. THIS was a horrible development.

The laughter carried on a little too long, so I decided to end it. I got to my feet, wiped the blood from my face, and said, "Happy I brought some levity to your day. Sure hope the uncalled for violence unleashed on me doesn't cause my concussion to worsen." I felt I was delivering a *gotcha* statement. They'd have to be concerned about my physical wellbeing, right?

The laughter stopped, and I thought my strategy had worked. I'd gained the upper hand. Then Master Sergeant

Lucas spoke. "Oh my God, you really were dropped on your head."

Well, I didn't see that one coming, and the refreshed round of laughter told me not one of them cared about my head. I need to surround myself with nicer people!

After an eternity of being the focal point of their amusement, the laughter finally ended. I glanced around the group, making sure they had gotten it out of their system before speaking. When all seemed calm, I turned a little more serious and asked, "Willis, have you talked to your family about the transfer?"

His expression told me he hadn't.

"Well, get moving. Time's a wasting. I'll show the master sergeant around and make introductions."

With a stiff nod, Willis retreated to his Hummer and started to pull away. He hit the brakes as he pulled even with me and said, "I need to talk to you. Stop by the house at fifteen hundred hours. That gives you two hours to show Lucas around." Not waiting for a response, he headed off to talk to his family.

After Willis left, I spun to face Lucas. Her aggressive posture and smug expression dared me to *take my best shot*. She was baiting me, goading me into a fight so she could open a can of whoop-ass on me. Well, I'm smarter than that. So I turned to Randy and said, "Randy, have fun showing Master Sergeant Lucas around. Make sure you introduce her to Lisa. I'm sure she'll want to meet the twin she was separated from at birth."

Not waiting for Randy to respond, I pivoted back to Lucas and said, "Good day, Master Sergeant." And with that, I stomped off to rejoin Devon.

Two hours later, I was leaning against Willis' Hummer outside his family's home. I didn't knock for fear of interrupting his time. After about fifteen minutes, I determined that his conversation wasn't going well and decided to leave. I scribbled a note on the hood of his grime-covered Hummer, telling him to catch up with me later. As I headed home, he yelled from an open window for me to hold up.

A few seconds later, he emerged from the front door and walked to the Hummer. He was clad in a tee-shirt and shorts, both struggling to cover his muscular frame. I'd never seen him in anything but full battle-rattle. The kid was massive. I realized how lucky I'd been that in all the times I'd pressed his buttons, I'd never found the one that activated his *punch Otto* mode.

"Jesus, Willis. Does the Army feed you steroids for breakfast?"

Willis smiled and said, "Not anymore. We got too big, and the Army started spending too much on steroid-sized uniforms. Now we get eggs and bacon."

The mention of the two most delicious breakfast foods ever created made my mouth water. It had been weeks since I'd grubbed a thick-cut piece of bacon let alone a fresh egg, over easy with rye toast. Note to self: Find some chickens and pigs to raise.

My eyes glazed over, imagining a table full of beautiful bacon. We'd been supplementing our diet with military-issued MREs and I missed fresh food.

Willis clicked his fingers in my face and shattered my daydream. I quickly checked my chin for drool but only found a five o'clock shadow. Whew!

"Thinking about bacon, Otto?"

I responded with a slow, sad nod.

"Well, I have something that'll cheer you up. Check it out." Willis opened the rear passenger door.

I stepped closer to the Hummer. Only seeing a large olive-drab canvas, I looked questioningly at Willis. Confused by my reaction, he turned to look into the backseat. "Sorry." He reached in and yanked the canvas from the Hummer.

The area was crammed with supplies. Not just any supplies – bang makers!

"Oh, Willis, it's all so beautiful. All mine?"

Willis chuckled and said, "No, Otto. Not all yours. You'll be sharing with the team and community. They fell off a supply truck directly into the back of my Humvee. It was the damnedest thing. I won't need them at Riley, so I figured you all could use them."

Water crept into my eyes; because my *allergies* were acting up. I tried to talk, but because of said allergies, my voice hitched in my throat.

Willis asked if I wanted a closer look. I responded with an overly enthusiastic nod. The first thing I wanted to touch was the stunningly beautiful M2 .50 caliber machinegun. I couldn't believe I'd get to fire the sexy beast affectionately called Ma-Deuce. An additional M249 was also a part of the stash. Six additional M4s, a dozen Sig-M17s, and a ton of ammo rounded out the stash.

Willis interrupted my reverence and said, "One more thing." He opened the passenger side front door, pulled out a large box and placed it at my feet.

Like a child on Christmas morning, I tore into it, seeking the treasure within. I wasn't sure how to react to the box's contents and shot Willis a puzzled glance. He smiled and said, "A little birdie told me you may need a better helmet. But remember, they only protect your head when you wear them."

The box was full of neatly stacked Enhanced Combat Helmets. He had a point, and the new helmets eliminated my excuse for not wearing one.

I locked eyes with Willis and said, "Thank you." But something important was missing. Being the ungrateful man that I am, I continued, "Your gift will go a long way in keeping us alive. But, and it's a big but, we need a vehicle, a Hummer to be exact."

"Otto, Otto, Otto, I didn't forget. You're standing in front of it. Lucas will pick me up and take me back to Hopkins. This baby is all yours. And it's called a Humvee."

Lucas' name ruined my mood and caused the cut on my forehead to throb. My mouth was moving before my brain could stop it, "Why her? Why is she replacing you?

She's … unpleasant. Actually, she's mean. And those eyes of hers, they make her look possessed."

"You know, Otto. Some people might say you're the unpleasant one. And I've peered into your eyes several times and found a lunatic staring back at me. Give her a chance."

"Lunatic? That's an overstatement, don't you think?"

Willis' silence answered my question, and I moved to cut off any further critiques of my personality. "Well, I guess it's time to take my insane self home." I stopped myself from storming away and reached out my hand. Willis grabbed it, and as we shook, I said, "I'll miss you. Be careful and rest easy knowing your family's safe."

"That's the only reason I'm able to leave, Otto. I know you'll do everything you can to protect them. One more thing: I didn't want to mention it in front of Lucas. They denied my request to end my enlistment. I'd figured as much. But I'm okay with it as long as my family's close by."

At a loss for words, I nodded and reaffirmed his family's safety in our community. I locked him in a hard stare. "Keep your head low and your hopes high … and I'll need the keys for the Hummer."

With a wink and a nod, our meeting ended.

CHAPTER 36
WASP ONE

James O'Brien had Jessica where he wanted her. No more games. Today he'd claim his prize. He stealthily entered the small supply closet while she searched for whatever item President Wharton had determined she couldn't live without.

"Hello, my sexy Jessica."

Jessica's shock morphed to horror when she identified the voice. She spun to face the vile man who'd trapped her. His lustful stare removed any hope she had of escaping.

"What was it you told me you'd do to me? Oh, I remember, you want to castrate me. Well, sexy Jessica, let's see what happens if you try."

The thought of this man having his way with her snapped something deep in her soul. Her fear of physical confrontation vanished. Jessica realized that she'd have to fight.

She reached to the small of her back, removing the dagger from its sheath under her blouse. The feel of the blade in her hand spurred her to action, and she lunged at the hulking man's throat.

James instantly realized his mistake; he had underestimated her capacity for violence. Pain streaked through his body as the blade entered his neck, severing his carotid artery.

His screams were drowned out by a massive explosion that rocked the yacht violently a moment later. Jessica had no time to register her action before another massive explosion sounded.

She jumped over the dying man and rushed to the deck. Fearing a boat in the flotilla had exploded, she worried that the devastation would soon spread to *The Flame*. The sight greeting her from the main deck confused her. Two sleek military aircraft were bombing Alameda Island, just across the bay.

President Wharton and Amanda soon joined Jessica on the main deck. Wharton spun into panic as she witnessed the destruction taking place a few miles away. "Those aren't our aircraft. RAM is attacking us! They must think I'm on the island."

Smoke from the attack traveled across the bay, engulfing the flotilla and stinging Wharton's eyes and turning them an evil red. Jessica glanced at Wharton just as a breeze blew through the woman's hair. She flinched at the sight; Wharton appeared to be losing her sanity.

She twisted away from the quickly unhinging president and rushed to the opposite side of the yacht. The entire population of the flotilla was watching the spectacle.

She understood that the mishmash of boats posed an easy target for the RAM aircraft. Panic in control, she considered jumping into the murky water, but then what?

Drowning in the bay seemed no less horrifying than being bombed from existence.

Resigned to her death, she slid to the deck and began sobbing. The deafening sound of the jets as they passed over the yacht caused her to raise her head. While she watched her death approach at supersonic speed, something incredible happened. The lead jet tipped its wings. She thought it was an optical illusion until the duo circled around and repeated the movement.

They might live one more day.

Bu Gang

The appearance of the Raptors sent a shock wave rippling through the crew of the *Bu Gang*. Packet ordered a full stop and commanded all personnel to take cover below deck. Soon after, the ship cut all power, plunging the lower decks into darkness. The *Bu Gang* now appeared to be just another derelict husk adrift under the Golden Gate Bridge.

Packet and Choke watched from the darkened bridge as the warplanes dropped a massive amount of ordnance on an unseen target.

Choke turned to Packet, eyes wide with hope, and said, "Wharton wasn't lying. Her military is still strong."

"It appears so," Packet answered with a suspicious tone. He continued, "Is she attempting to clear the area for our arrival?"

Choke hadn't considered the implications of the attack. Why would Wharton squander resources on what amounted to a fool's errand? Doubt settled in, then suddenly Packet pointed excitedly at the aircraft. Choke glanced to the sky just in time to see the lead Raptor tip its wings.

He exclaimed, "That's it. She's letting us know the area is clear."

The men beamed. The pieces were falling into place. The warplanes roared overhead, circled the bay, and accelerated. Their afterburners shone brightly as they quickly disappeared into the eastern sky.

Unable to control his eagerness, Packet screamed, "Radio for the helicopters to prepare for battle."

Wasp One

"Wasp One, repeat your transmission."

"This is Wasp One. I say again, a large number of civilian vessels are moored together south of Hunters Point. We signaled them that we are aware of their location. Additionally, North Korean Navy vessels are present in San Francisco Bay. Awaiting orders to engage the enemy."

"Wasp One, this is Davis Air Command. Hold for direction."

Lieutenant Colonel Cloy shook his head in disbelief. How had those snakes avoided The Seventh Fleet? It didn't matter now, they were here.

Cloy quickly delivered his orders. "Return to base. We cannot risk losing them. Deploy a UAV to recon the area."

He stared at the large wall-mounted monitors following the dots that represented his men. This unexpected development weighed on his mind as he whispered, "If you're looking for a fight, you found one. But you are not prepared for the violence we are capable of."

CHAPTER 37
LEVEL TWO

Doctor McCune poured over the data from the human trials. Unknown hours had ticked away since they had administered the antidote to the volunteers.

They'd quarantined the surviving test subjects under heavy guard in the hospital cafeteria. McCune was denied access to them due to the threat of another violent outbreak. The military deemed him too important to risk being killed.

Blood was being drawn and tested at a frenetic clip. The subjects' vitals were recorded every fifteen minutes. The area bustled with activity.

An amazing trend had emerged. The antidote was having a healing effect on the subjects suffering from terminal illnesses. Of particular interest was Ben Reyes. His blood test indicated that his cancer had vanished. McCune ordered an MRI and anxiously awaited the results.

Doctor McCune had started reviewing the mountain of data for a third time when Sergeant Timmons entered his office.

The gruff soldier announced his presence by ordering the doctor to follow him. His posture was such that McCune obeyed without question.

Anxiety coursing through him, McCune asked, "Has another outbreak occurred?"

"No. Just follow me and don't speak. You can thank me later."

The cloak and dagger routine annoyed the doctor. If Timmons was wasting his time, there'd be hell to pay.

McCune prepared to demand an explanation when Sims suddenly stopped in front of the UC holding cells.

"I overheard your conversation. You needed to test a level two. Now you have three."

McCune spun and peered through the observation window. Three UCs lay secured to gurneys, with nebulizers already releasing the antidote into the room. Doctor Kris paced the area, donning a hazmat suit, recording vitals, and observing the subjects' reactions.

The level two monsters were frightening. Their rasping was unsettling, but the way they worked their hands in what appeared to be an attempt to escape the thick straps securing their wrists caused McCune's teeth to grind.

Engrossed in the proceedings, he flinched when Timmons spoke. "Doctor, I have information regarding the human test subjects. One of them eluded my men. They didn't realize one was missing until they found its carcass an hour after the outbreak ended." Timmons paused and pivoted to face the doctor before continuing, "It had concealed itself behind a bank of monitors."

McCune was confused. "Forgive me if my question appears ignorant, but why is this important? The test subjects suffering the reaction displayed clear reasoning skills. They hadn't reverted to mindless monsters. So its ability to determine it should hide is not surprising."

"Doctor, they found it in a pool of its own bodily fluids. It appeared deflated … literally deflated. The antidote dissolved everything but its skin."

Although shocked by the revelation, McCune didn't consider it bad news. In fact, it was excellent news. It meant that any living being susceptible to the reaction only lived for a short period after the reaction took hold. Coupled with the fact that they weren't infectious and therefore couldn't spread the condition to others, their destructive impact was limited to the time it took for the antidote to destroy their bodies.

McCune succumbed to a feeling he hadn't experienced in weeks. Hope! A smile creased his exhausted features. He started to answer Timmons' questioning stare when something crashed against the observation window.

Both men reacted to the sound by snapping their heads towards the window. Confusion and fear jolted through McCune when he realized he could no longer see into the room. Blood, now smeared across the window, obscured his view. The screams reached his ears a moment later.

McCune gasped and instinctively stepped back as the gore dripped away, giving him a hazy view of the room's interior. He screamed, "NO, this can't be! Sergeant, do something."

Timmons' response crushed the doctor. "She's already dead."

The sergeant began barking orders into his shoulder-mounted radio. The sounds of boots slapping the tiled floor soon followed.

McCune watched in transfixed horror as one of the level two UCs held Doctor Kris' severed head in the air, greedily gulping the blood pouring from her neck.

Tears blurred his vision, mercifully obscuring his sight. But the scene had already burnt into his memory. His friend was dead.

The pieces collided in his mind. He ran from the ghastly scene, pushing past the soldiers responding to Timmons' orders. McCune broke through the human roadblock and rushed to his office. He entered the small space and searched frantically for the phone. The seconds that passed felt like hours as his fear grew.

Finally locating it, he selected the only number the phone ever called. When the line picked up, he screamed, "We mustn't move forward. Whatever you do, do not release the antidote. Its reaction in level two subjects will prove devastating to humanity. They achieve the same aggression levels as the human test subjects. But it doesn't cure them of the virus – it enhances the virus. We've created an incredibly advanced UC!"

The ice-cold response threatened to steal his sanity. "Good doctor, you're far too late. The package is en route."

CHAPTER 38
LET THEM HAVE IT

Chairman Mallet glared at the bank of wall monitors as the analyst highlighted the flotilla and the DPRK fleet's location. The satellite images being reviewed were now several weeks old, and she presented the information as approximates based on the F22 pilots' information. It equated to *best guess intelligence.*

When the analyst finished her briefing, Mallet dismissed her and swiveled his chair to face the Joint Chiefs of Staff's remaining members.

"Our UAV will enter the bay area in approximately two hours. We must develop a strategy and contingency before it arrives. Suggestions?"

Mallet's assistant interrupted. "Sir, First Lieutenant Billings, from Camp Hopkins, is requesting to speak with you. It's urgent and pertains to Senator Shafter."

Mallet gave a stiff nod and said, "Patch him through the speakers."

A moment later, Billings' voice filled the room. "Chairman Mallet, First Lieutenant Billings. I'll cut to the chase. We have taken Senator Shafter into custody. He refuses to speak to anyone but you, Sir."

Mallet rubbed at his temples while answering. "If that blowhard intends to waste my time, let him know we will redeposit him in the middle of Lake Erie, with haste."

"Understood, Sir. I'll retrieve him ASAP."

After an extended pause, the unreasonably confident voice of Senator Shafter sprang from the speakers. "I must begin by expressing my disappointment with you and your people for their lackluster treatment of a duly appointed senator. I'm a head of state, for God's sake. But your people are handling me as if I'm a common criminal."

Mallet was in no mood and shut Shafter down immediately. "I agree. You're not a common criminal. You are, in fact, a traitor." He paused, ensuring his statement had firmly locked Shafter's jaw. It had. So he continued, "You told me you had INTEL. Start talking."

"Chairman Mallet, I refuse to speak until after I'm fed and bathed. I'll also need to see my quarters to ensure they are on par with my position."

Mallet shook his head in disbelief. "Billings, execute the good senator within the hour."

Shafter's crumbling voice spoke over Billings' response. "MALLET, hold on. I'll tell you everything. Just cancel that order."

"Shafter, start talking."

"President Wharton is located in San Francisco Bay. I possess no information regarding additional inhabitants of her flotilla. But she relayed her location to me. I'm giving it to Billings as we speak. Also, she alone colluded with North

Korea on the development of the virus. I became aware of her role moments before RAM bombed the Sea Cliff. I was traveling to join her flotilla, at which time I planned to execute her. It's obvious that I failed in my quest. But my intent was noble."

Mallet met the surprised looks of the joint chiefs; now they knew who was afloat off Hunters Point. More importantly, they understood why the DPRK was steaming into the Bay.

Mallet determined that they needed no other information. "Billings, please show the *noble* senator to his quarters. And be sure his *assistant* is present. I'm sure they'll have a great deal to discuss."

Mallet could hear the smile on Shafter's face when he spoke. "Thank you, Chairman Mallet. I'm pleased to hear that you recognize my value, and I await the opportunity to speak with you in depth. I'm an asset to any committee and look forward to joining your ranks. Please inform President Train I'm available for consultations."

Mallet disconnected the transmission, leaned back in his chair, and said, "Ladies and gentlemen. I believe our best course of action against the threat is no action. Let them have it."

Admiral Gilroy spoke first. "Sir, I'm not sure I follow. We can't allow a hostile force to infiltrate our country. Especially now. Our resources are near their breaking point."

Mallet smiled and said, "Exactly, Admiral. That's why we'll let the DPRK deal with Wharton and the UC hordes. Our UAV will determine if any of their subs traveled with them. If they have, we move immediately. If not, we let them link with Wharton. Once the C130s drop the antidote, the bay will be under constant observation. They won't make a single move without us knowing."

Mallet paused, letting understanding wash through the joint chiefs. He continued. "My guess is that the DPRK will quickly determine that Wharton wields no power. After which they'll eliminate her and move to invade BSU. An invasion will require them to land on the shores of one of the most heavily infested cities on earth." After an effectual pause, he continued. "It'll be entertaining to watch."

Shafter felt power seeping back into his body. He was confident that President Train would welcome him back into the command structure. *I'm far too valuable.* It was only a matter of time. A matter of feeding Mallet the most damaging intelligence he possessed about his beloved Blue States United.

Billings' voice pulled Shafter from his daydream as he commanded someone named Albright to escort him to his quarters.

"Yes, Albright. I'm looking forward to seeing my office. I'll need a meal delivered to me after I shower away this filth."

Albright's laugh caught him by surprise, and he fought the instinct to lash out at the soldier. *Not yet, not until I'm fully integrated.*

"Senator Shafter, follow me. I'll take you to your *office* and have a fresh suit delivered to you. Does that sound appropriate?"

Shafter's crooked grin appeared. "Very fitting, young man. Please lead the way."

The walk to his office was quiet. *Soldier boy is intimidated by my presence; understandable, considering who I am.*

As they walked further into the bowels of Camp Hopkins, Shafter grew agitated. The windowless area resembled a prison more than an area set up for offices, not to mention appropriate living quarters.

When Albright unbuckled a heavily laden key chain from a strap on his chest-rig, Shafter picked up his pace. He intended to stand under a scalding hot shower until the grime of the last six weeks melted from his body.

Albright glanced over his shoulder and said, "Well, here we are. I hope you find it up to your standards. We aim to please at Camp Hopkins."

The amused tone in Albright's voice made Shafter uneasy. His jaw hinged open to question the soldier, but the appearance of a large steel door with a heavily armed soldier standing in front of it cut his thought short.

Albright stopped abruptly and said, "After you, Mister Senator."

Shafter continued forward but quickly realized what was happening. He attempted to turn and run, but Albright had deftly positioned himself behind him, blocking his only exit.

Albright tossed the keys to the guard and ordered him to unlock the door, then took hold of Shafter's neck, forcing him into the room. He gave the senator a stiff shove the moment he crossed the threshold.

Shafter spun and attempted to force his way past Albright and out of the room only to land hard on his back, gasping for air.

"Senator Shafter. We hope you find your accommodations meet your high standards. Five-star service is our goal at Camp Hopkins. Regrettably, you'll share your quarters with your assistant, whom you'll find sleeping on the bunk in the corner. Please let us know ... oh, to hell with it. You, Sir, are a prisoner of war and will be treated accordingly."

Albright slammed and locked the door. The single light hanging from the ceiling cast the edges of the room in a shadowy darkness. Shafter could make out a human form sitting motionless in a corner. He panicked, thinking they had placed him in a room with one of the monsters.

As he cowered against the door, a familiar voice pierced the shadows. "Dear Senator, have you chosen the parts of your body you can live without?"

CHAPTER 39
STILL UNHAPPY

Pat glared at me when I entered her house. I made sure I arrived at exactly five o'clock. I didn't see any reason to fan the flames of her anger. And considering I was already on her list because of the incident earlier in the day, behaving myself seemed the better plan. So I arrived on time.

The community's de facto leadership already crowded the room. I scurried to Darline's side and sat next to her.

It became apparent, rather quickly, that Pat was still unhappy with me. "Nice of you to join us, Mister Hammer."

"What? I'm on time. Actually, I'm a few seconds early."

"Otto, the meeting starts at five. That means you arrive a couple minutes before five. We're busy people and can't afford to waste our time waiting for your royal highness to arrive."

I saw where this was heading. So, choosing to spare myself a verbal beat down, I apologized ... but I didn't mean it.

The meeting's topic was something we were all worried about. How would we survive through the winter? To date, everything had been running as smoothly as one could expect during an apocalypse. Water and power were functioning, with backup plans for both. But it was those very subjects Pat wanted to review.

"Vice President Pace identified two areas of concern. Slow reaction time to power outages and a looming shortage of natural gas. Ninety percent of our homes use natural gas for heat and cooking. How do we react when the supply is cut off?"

The room fell silent. Of all the things I'd been worried about, heating my home wasn't one of them. Thoughts of wearing seven pairs of socks and four sweaters raced around my head. Not to mention no hot water for showers. What would happen if a water line broke? How would we heat our food?

Anxiety seeped into my body, then an idea hit me. I barked out my idea at the same time it entered my head, "Propane!"

Apparently, my proclamation cut Pat off mid-sentence. Every single person in the room stared at me. Pat, however, shot daggers at me. I waited for someone to pick up the conversation, to concur, or support me in any way. But the sissies just gawked at me. So I took the lead.

"We convert the natural gas homes to propane. Easy-peasy. FST1 can secure the conversion kits, propane, and any accessories."

It was a good idea, hard work, dangerous, and time-consuming, but still a good idea. Nonetheless, Pat wanted me to prove it. "Who, pray tell, will be tasked with converting each and every house in the community to propane?"

"Well, Pat, I'm sure the kits come with directions. We gather up anyone with electrical or plumbing backgrounds and set them loose."

She stood in front of the group and gave up her fight. She asked, "What does everyone think. I'd like to stop Otto from prattling on. So let's vote on his suggestion."

Twenty minutes later, after solving yet another crisis, Darline and I stood in our driveway admiring the team's new Hummer.

"She's a beauty, isn't she?"

"Yep, she really is." The voice didn't belong to Darline. I spun to find Randy staring fixedly at the beast of a vehicle.

Darline, apparently not as excited about the Hummer, had already gone inside, leaving me in the driveway alone until Randy arrived.

"Hey, check out the backseat. Most of them are for Dillan to assign to the guards, but I wanted to enjoy them a bit longer. They're so damned beautiful."

Randy gave a whistle when he got a peek at the military-grade goodies. "That's an M2, Otto! With ammo!" After a long silence, he said, "Otto, we need to let the team know what you just volunteered them for. This isn't like the plan to run the UCs over with the dump trucks. It will take multiple missions outside the walls to secure enough supplies to implement your plan. Not to mention, I'm out of commission and you're borderline. But I have an idea."

Randy shared his thoughts in rapid-fire order. When he finished, he asked my thoughts. As I opened my mouth to answer, he said, "Actually, Otto. I wasn't asking, I'm telling you. Andy is taking my place. I've already told him. For now, you and I will hold down the fort." He locked me in a challenging stare and said, "Good, I'm glad you agree. The mission starts in forty-eight hours. I'll let the team know. Oh, and I'll be taking the M2 with me for a cleaning and inspection."

CHAPTER 40
LEADING EDGE

Bobby had chosen this location for a simple reason: the landscape. The heavily wooded area would provide cover for his troops as they approached their target. Surprise was vital for his plan to succeed.

He soon realized his position afforded him an unobstructed view into a large swath of the compound, including two of their watchtowers. The east-to-west layout of the streets would allow him to kill their residents as they exited their homes and attempted to join the fight.

"This is perfect."

"*Don't get cocky. They've proven to be worthy adversaries. You shouldn't underestimate their ability to defend themselves.*"

"Herbert, trust me. My plan will bring us the victory we so rightfully deserve. Our army will arrive soon. Prepare for the battle to come."

The raspy sound of the dead reached his ears. The leading edge of his army had arrived. It wouldn't be long before the air was filled with the screams of the dying as his troops tore them apart.

Bobby's excitement grew when his attention was drawn to a pair of military vehicles preparing to exit the community. He broke into uncontrollable laughter as he watched their best fighters drive away.

It was all coming together!

Chapter 41
Send Off

Willis' Hummer arrived at the gate first, with Master Sergeant Lucas behind the wheel. I leaned into the open passenger side window and met Willis' stare. I would miss him. We'd been working together since the second day of the apocalypse, and I'd grown to trust him.

"Whelp," I started, "you're really leaving us."

His patented smile on full display, Willis said, "Only for a quick minute, Otto. I'll be back before you know it."

Lucas leaned forward and, with a wicked grin, said, "Isn't this precious. Are you going to kiss Sergeant Willis goodbye?"

"Excuse me, Master Sergeant, but are you having sexual fantasies about me? Is that why you want to see me kiss Sergeant Willis? I can't blame you, if you are. I have that effect on women." I watched the blood rise from her neck to about mid-way up her face. Her reaction would have caused most people to pull back on their banter. I'm not most people. Plus, I found her to be abrasive, so I continued, "Oh, I know. You want to kiss me, right?"

I was impressed when the blood filling her face reached just past her eyes. Her reaction spurred me on. "Well, I know this may break your little black heart, but Missus Hammer wouldn't take kindly to that. However, if things don't work out at home, you'll be the first woman I call."

I shifted my focus back to Willis, who stared at me with something approaching wonderment. But not like a little kid at Disney World – more like the wonderment one experiences in witnessing a terrible accident, like an eighteen-wheeler versus a bicycle. So what I'm trying to say, is shock.

I smiled at him and said, "Good luck. Wait; am I not supposed to wish a soldier good luck? Shit, man, did I jinx you?"

"Don't worry, Otto. And thanks."

"And I meant what I said about your family."

Willis gave me a nod and turned to face the windshield. I looked at Lucas and winked. Lucas' gloved fist twitched, so I quickly pulled away from the window and waved them through the gate.

Randy, never one for goodbyes, saluted them as they passed him. He respected Willis, and a salute was his way of showing the soldier how he felt.

My stomach clenched when the team pulled up. I fought the urge to climb into the Hummer and join the mission. But I was still a liability. I was getting better, but the effects of my concussion continued to dance *around the edges*. And slamming my head off the street to avoid Lucas' right hook hadn't helped with my recovery. My presence could jeopardize the entire team.

Wait a minute, I only counted four heads. Lisa's smiling face was missing.

Dillan joined me and said, "Before you go full tilt, Lisa isn't feeling well this morning. Woke up feeling nauseous, and it went hard south from there. The sounds coming from the bathroom were frightening. She wants to lie low for a few days; make sure she isn't coming down with something contagious. I think it's the nasty MRE she ate last night, but she wanted to play it safe."

Dillan's explanation didn't make it any better. When Randy joined us, it was obvious he wasn't happy either. His expression full of concern, he turned to the team and said, "Four isn't enough. I was skittish with five. My vote is we scrap the mission until we can mount a full team."

I jumped in, "I'm with Randy."

The team bristled at our trepidation. They received it as a lack of confidence in their ability. But that wasn't the issue. The more people covering your back, the more likely you come home alive. Four people weren't enough!

Will glanced around at the determined faces in the Hummer and said, "The team voted that we go. Our community is counting on us."

"Hey," I started. "No one voted!"

"Yeah, but no one agreed with you either. Open the gate."

Dillan removed a folded piece of paper from his shirt pocket. He handed it to Will and said, "We need a better antenna for the radio. We've contacted other survivors, but our signal's weak. I wrote down what we need. If you come across one, grab it if possible."

The gate opened, and FST1 began their mission as Randy and I looked on.

CHAPTER 42
RED GLARE

Jessica watched the North Korean air-cushioned landing craft speed away from *The Flame*. They'd arrived shortly after the barrage of Alameda Island ended and proved nearly as devastating as the bombs dropped on the island city.

Wharton had lied to the North Koreans about Blue States United's military capabilities. She thought she'd have more time to develop a strategy to deal with them; to determine a way to use the DPRK's resources to strike back at Right America.

But when the DPRK delegation members questioned Wharton about the military action they had witnessed, they quickly uncovered her deceit. The one named Packet ordered their soldiers to take the president into custody and threatened death to anyone resisting their actions.

With James dead, they found themselves at the mercy of the DPRK. The group watched helplessly as Wharton was whisked away. Jessica had expected the fiery woman to go kicking and screaming. Instead, Wharton appeared resigned to her fate and boarded their landing craft, her shoulders slumped in defeat.

The remaining political hacks ignored the fact that the DPRK helicopters remained overhead long after the landing craft disappeared from sight. Instead, they immediately began jockeying for the leadership position created by Wharton's departure. It was pathetic.

As the red glare emitted from the lead helicopter's side, it became clear why they had remained. A slight smile broke on Jessica's face as she braced for death.

Chapter 43
Rocky River

Jackson wasn't enjoying my company, but I had no place else to go. Randy had stormed off after FST1 left the gate, Darline was inventorying supplies with Pat, and Dillan went home to check on Lisa. So Jackson drew the short straw.

His displeasure with me wasn't my fault. He could have avoided it if he had been performing his job more efficiently.

Jackson had been working on up-armoring the dump trucks. Well, *working* may be an overstatement. Therein laid the problem. Jackson just didn't seem engaged, so I attempted to encourage him to pick up the pace. He was close to completing the first of the two trucks. But at this rate it would be next summer before he finished the second one.

He had been welding a section of rebar to its metal anchors on the truck's frame. But he kept shifting to his backside while performing the task. It looked like he was taking a break every fifteen minutes.

So I told him, "Hey, you're giving the Hammers a bad name."

Sweat and grime rolled down his face when he looked up to find me supervising his work, "Otto, go away. Didn't you already get chewed out for providing *field guidance?*"

"Oh, Jacky, you're so clever or witty, maybe both. But it's not helping you work any faster. And those attachment points of yours are pathetic. Who taught you how to weld?"

"Otto, you see the gun in my holster, right?"

"I do, but I've also seen you shoot, so I like my chances."

Jackson struggled to his feet and began a slow, menacing walk in my direction. He started mumbling empty threats under his breath as he halved the distance. It surprised me. I figured he'd try to shoot me, but it looked like he wanted to beat me into silence. Rookie move!

Still salty about the day's events, I decided a barroom brawl may be just what the doctor ordered. I squared up and got ready for his standard left jab fake, followed by a brutal right cross.

When he closed to within striking distance, my radio squawked to life, "Dillan for Otto."

I signaled Jackson to *hold on* and answered Dillan, "Go for Otto."

"I need you in the Radio Room, pronto. It's set up in the basement of Jax's house."

The mention of Jax tugged at my emotions. It reminded me of the world we now lived in and how any one of us could be gone in an instant. I looked at my brother and apologized. He gave a stiff nod and spun away. He wasn't over it, but he no longer wanted to take my life ... baby steps.

"On my way. What's with the urgency?"

"We've contacted another community. They requested to speak with you by name."

"Huh. I'm not sure how I feel about that. See you in two."

A minute thirty seconds later I was talking to a man named Olaf. And the conversation was an eye opener.

"So, I'm finally talking to the legend himself," Olaf said.

"Well, that's a bit strong. But yes, I'm the legend named Otto Hammer." I had already forgotten his last name. I continued, "So, Olaf. Tell me. How do you know my name? I don't recall knowing an Olaf. Enlighten me."

"We've been monitoring your radio chatter for weeks."

The revelation floored me.

When I didn't respond, Olaf shared some information I wouldn't soon live down. "Sometimes, when you got really fired up, we gathered around the radio to listen. It was better than reality television." A hearty laugh followed!

I eyeballed Dillan, who looked as shocked as me. It was obvious we shared the same thought: *Who else was monitoring our radio chatter?* My mind kicked into overdrive as I tried to recall every single radio transmission made by the community. *Had we ever talked about our location? Did we talk about our force size? What about conversations regarding our weapons and other supplies?* The list was long and sent chills down my spine.

With as much calm as I could muster, I said, "Well, you have me at a disadvantage. Tell me more about you and your community. Are you interested in opening up trade?"

I released the talk button and asked Dillan if Olaf appeared on the list of communities the VP had given us after his speech. He wasn't. Not good!

Olaf answered, and frankly he spooked me. It felt like he was in the room listening to Dillan and I talk. "If you're wondering, you won't find us on the contact list from the government. I never had much use for them. Nor trusted them all that much. But that doesn't mean you shouldn't trust us. And yes, we want to start trading with you."

"I think I might like you, Olaf. We think alike. So, what's your offer?" I knew it would happen; We The People were taking our first steps towards rebuilding our country!

"Well, Otto. You'll need to run this by Pat," he said while snickering. "We need access to your medics. My boy took a fall; his leg's a mess. We could really use some help. I ... I can't lose my boy, Otto." His sincerity disarmed me.

I rattled through the logic. *If he meant us harm, he had enough information about us to have already done so. If he wanted to rob us, he would have asked for a tangible item and robbed us when we met.* His back was against the wall. He just needed our help.

"Well, Olaf. It wouldn't be very neighborly of us not to help your son." I used the conversation to probe him for INTEL. "Can your boy travel? If so, do you know our location?"

Olaf's voice filled with hope, "That, Otto, is something you all never talked about. We have a general idea. He can travel, but he's in no shape for a long journey. I understand the need for caution. So, if I tell you our location, will you tell me yours?"

He was saying all the right things. I glanced back at Dillan, and he nodded. Like me, he understood that with growth comes risk. And eventually, we needed to take a chance on someone.

"Olaf, let's help your son. What's your location?"

"We've taken over the nature center in the Rocky River Branch of the Metro Parks."

I knew that place well. I used to tell Darline it would be the perfect place to hole up if an apocalypse ever hit. Guess I wasn't the only one who recognized its potential!

"I'm very familiar with the area. Are you using Fort Hill, or just the center?"

"The nature center for housing. We use Fort Hill for observing the area. It's been quiet since day one; only a few stragglers have shown up. Zombies aren't much into nature, I guess."

"That's what I figured, Olaf. It was a brilliant choice. We're located in the Deerfield Subdivision."

"I know the area, Otto. When can we bring my boy?"

"I'll talk to Durrell and Sabrina, and as you mentioned, Pat. We'll radio back after ..."

Pat's voice cut in, "Bring him now. What's your ETA?"

It surprised me that Pat was so eager to allow Olaf to enter our community. I guess we were all ready for the next step in taking back our world.

Pat explained our entry policy and told him which gate he needed to enter through. She told Dillan to direct the guards to radio her directly when Olaf arrived.

Then Olaf said something that almost made me cry. "Can you safely store around a hundred pounds of venison? I'll offer it as payment."

Fresh meat! I couldn't believe it, he has fresh meat! I jumped at the offer. "We do. But we were planning on helping your son, regardless."

"I figured as much, but I can't let you do that. We'll load everything up and see you in an hour. I'm driving a Ram 1500, black with a bed-cap. Otto, Pat, Dillan ... thank you."

After the conversation ended, I turned to Dillan and said, "Nobody needs to hear about the *reality TV* comment."

CHAPTER 44
SHOPPING LIST

Will backed the Hummer to the doors of the big-box hardware store. It was the first one on their list, and their best chance for finding the propane conversion kits.

"Tesha, did Dillan put anything on his list other than parts for the antenna?"

She unfolded the paper, took a quick read, and answered, "No. He asked only for the antenna. Nothing else."

He nodded. "Let's roll. Tesha, you're with me. Andy, you're with Stone. Do not break formation. No gunfire unless absolutely necessary." He looked at each team member, then asked, "We ready?" He received three stiff nods in reply.

The wrecked sliding doors allowed easy access to the store. Its interior resembled the war-torn streets of Iraq. Shelves were toppled, destroyed merchandise covered the floor, and bodies littered the aisles. Apparently, the virus had roared through this building, catching dozens of shoppers in its web.

Three feet into the store, Will said, "Andy, grab a shopping cart. Stone, stay on Andy's six." The men moved without question, and soon they were traversing the debris-covered floor deep into the bowels of the store.

As the ambient light faded, weapon-mounted lights clicked on, piercing the oppressive darkness. As the team rounded the corner of the plumbing and HVAC aisles, a sound reached them. Faint at first, it rapidly grew louder.

Will threw his fist in the air, signaling a stop. They stood motionless, straining to identify the slapping sound coming from deeper within the store.

Realization hit them seconds before the source came into view. Countless UCs charged their position from the far end of the aisle. Will barked, "Back to the Hummer. Move!"

Stone, now on point, his Tavor X95 leading the way, they retraced their path to the front of the store.

Andy nearly crashed into Stone when he came to a hard stop. Against the backdrop of sunlight shining through the doors, dozens of shambling monsters now blocked their exit.

"Exit is blocked," Stone yelled. "Heading for the second entrance."

As soon as the team entered the aisle leading to their alternate exit, Stone's Tavor rattled to life. They were surrounded.

CHAPTER 45
TYRANTS

Doctor Flocci smiled. He couldn't help himself. His work would soon be completed. Three more calls and it would all come together.

He pressed the send button and waited. When answered, he said, "Mister President. The human trials were successful. We have a green light to release the antidote over Alameda Island. The C130s are airborne as we speak."

President Train's voice bellowed through the small speaker. "Glorious news, fantastic news. I knew we'd beat the virus back. How long until we declare the Alameda test successful? It needs to happen quickly, Doctor. Quickly."

Flocci mustered all of his self-control; he hated this man and what he stood for. Being responsible for Train's failure would be the greatest accomplishment of his life. The doctor said, "Within a week. We'll identify if the delivery system is effective."

Train cut him off. "Wait, you said it worked in aerosol form. Why is it still in question? Did something change, Doctor? I need to know if something changed. Talk to me. What happened?"

"Relax, Mister President. We simply need to observe its use on a mass-scale. That's all."

"Okay. I trust you, Doctor, keep your foot on the gas! The world is depending on you!"

A reptilian smile creased Flocci's features before he responded, "Oh, I assure you, Mister President. My foot is firmly on the gas."

When the call with Train ended, the doctor immediately made the second of his three calls. This one promised to be the highlight of his day. When McCune's exhausted voice answered, Flocci went on the offensive. "You have undoubtedly discovered the healing potential of the antidote. A development that must remain under wraps until we study it further."

He paused to enjoy the panicked breathing emanating from the speaker. When McCune attempted to speak, Flocci stepped on his words, "To ensure the information doesn't get prematurely disseminated, I have arranged for your sequestration with me at CDC headquarters. Your escort will arrive within the hour. Good day, Doctor."

The power Flocci wielded was intoxicating. He quickly placed his third and final call. His anxiety grew with every second his call went unanswered. He checked his Rolex, confirming he was calling at exactly the specified time. Agitated, he disconnected and muttered, "Worthless politician. Answer your phone!" Then it hit him. The voicemail hadn't picked up. Nervously he pushed redial and waited. Again, nothing happened.

Anger surged through him. He shot to his feet, walked to the front of his desk and tried again. This time, he listened to dead air. The phone didn't even ring. His anger sent him into an uncontrolled rant. "This isn't happening. Limitless power and billions of dollars are at stake. Where are you? What has HAPPENED?"

Twenty-five hundred miles away, at the bottom of San Francisco Bay, a satellite phone went dark.

CHAPTER 46
PATRIOTS

My steps were quick and light. I'd allowed excitement to take over. We'd reached a turning point. We would soon be trading with another group and eating fresh meat. I couldn't stop thinking about it. Maybe, just maybe, we'd find another group to trade for bacon. Delicious bacon!

The residents of the community gawked at me as I passed them on my way home. I was waving and greeting them with a huge smile – both behaviors entirely out of character for me. Well, if my outward actions caught them off guard, they would have fainted at what was going on in my head.

I started up my drive when movement on Tesha's front porch caught my attention. It was Devon, notebook in hand.

"Hey, little man. What's the good word?"

Devon's surprised expression indicated he, too, was shocked by my behavior. He waved at me but didn't smile. Seemingly, he was worried I had slipped into insanity.

"Hey, I'm coming over. Hold on a second," I yelled while trotting in his direction.

He took a few steps and met me on the walkway to his porch. With big eyes and a smile slowly appearing on his face, he said, "Mister Otto, why are you smiling so much?"

"Devon, today is a great day. Remember it, write it down in your notebook. Today, we start to rebuild our country!"

The pavement in front of Devon exploded. He yelped in pain and slammed to the ground. The sound of his skull bouncing off the concrete reached my ears the same instant as the gun's report. When I bent over to check on him, the angry buzz of a bullet zipped over my head.

The realization of what was happening sank in. On auto-pilot, I scooped Devon up and bolted for his house as concrete shattered around us.

I kicked at the door and screamed, "May, open the door. We're being shot at."

The door burst open, and Devon's panicked aunt grabbed my arm, yanking me into the house. I rushed to the living room and laid Devon on the couch.

When I looked at my hand, something inside me broke. Blood dripped from my fingers.

I looked up, meeting May's horrified eyes, "May, radio Sabrina. Tell her to get here ASAP."

I didn't wait to see if she followed my command before I spun and headed for the door. The community was already in chaos. People scrambled for cover in every direction, some clutching blood-soaked wounds.

I grabbed my radio and barked, "All Towers, where are the shots coming from? Can any of you provide covering fire?"

Static filled the air. Another shot blasted into the ground to my right. I screamed into the radio, "Towers, guards, anyone, what's happening?"

A weak voice answered me. "This is Northeast Tower. Southeast Tower has been neutralized. I've been hit but can still fight. I'm pinned down though."

"This is Patrol One. We have eyes on hundreds of UCs approaching the barrier. We're holed up near Southeast Tower and have taken fire."

I was running toward the east gate when Dillan's voice broke over the radio. "Patrol One, engage the UC. Patrol Two, get into position and start sending rounds into the surrounding homes."

I broke in. "Dillan, this is Otto. The sound took a second or so longer than the bullet to reach me. The shots are coming from further out. Adjust Patrol Two's Fire."

"This is Patrol One. I glassed the area and caught a scope-glint in a second-story window at about a thousand yards away."

I needed the exact location; I intended to end this on my terms. "Patrol One. Tighten up that location."

Nothing but static.

"I say again, Patrol One, can you narrow the location?"

A different voice answered, "Otto, Becky's down. She didn't identify the location before being hit. We're taking direct fire. Unable to provide visual confirmation of shooter's location."

"Otto, this is Northeast Tower. I have a visual confirmation. Brick duplex, green shutters. Eight hundred yards due east of the gate. Otto, the area is swarming with UCs. Thousands of them. They're concentrating on the east barrier."

We'd gone from hundreds of UC to thousands in seconds. This was going sideways fast.

I soon detected a pattern. The enemy shots were random bursts of one or two and in strategic areas. This indicated a single shooter. Two at most. But one of them was an excellent shot, and his attack was eliciting the desired reactions. Fear and confusion.

"Northeast Tower, if you can. Focus your fire on that house."

Dillan's voice broke over the radio. "Patrol One, status on Becky?"

"Negative on Becky. I want this son-of-bitch dead."

Gunfire erupted from the community but it came in fits and starts as they were continually forced to take cover from the deadly sniper outside our gate. We would be overrun if we couldn't mount a sustained defense.

With the UCs clustering on our east barrier, an idea jumbled together in my head. I barked into the radio, "This bullshit ends now. I'm heading for the north barrier. Have a ladder ready for me."

Randy's voice screamed from the radio, "Otto, stop. We can neutralize the shooter from here."

"Randy, I can't make that shot, and you're in no condition to make it either. I got this. Bring Ma-Deuce to the party."

I broke hard left and headed for the north barrier and away from the main herd.

Eight Hundred Yards Away

"There! He's heading north. Shoot him!"

After neutralizing three targets and wounding another half dozen, Bobby bristled at Herbert telling him who or when to shoot. Especially when it came to the old man. "He'd already be dead if you hadn't bumped my hand."

"Your hands are twitching, Bobby Smith. Maybe you do need your medication."

"Shut your vile moth, Herbert. My army needs my covering fire. Let the coward run. My troops will find him no matter where he hides."

North Barrier

Adrenaline dumped into my system as I raced towards the ladder at the north barrier. When my foot hit the bottom rung, Darline's voice broke over the radio chatter.

"Otto Hammer, this is your wife. Whatever it is you're planning, stop!"

I came down hard on the boulders positioned outside the rammed earth section of the barrier. Still, I stayed on my feet and mercifully avoided breaking an ankle. The area was thick with monsters. They were getting hung up in our defensive obstacles, but the bodies began stacking up. The fallen carcasses created a slimy pathway for the trailing UCs to follow directly to our home.

I needed to move, but first, I answered Darline. "I'll be home for dinner, chick. I promise."

"Don't you do this to me, Otto Hammer. Please don't!" Her voice was strained with fear. It was too late. I had already committed to my hastily assembled plan.

"I love you, babe. You will live through this. We all will. Now, get to the east barrier and kill these bastards. We can't allow them to overrun our home."

I clipped the radio to my belt and glanced back at the cyclone fence section of the barrier. The pike teams were manning their positions, but no citizens lined the rammed earth barrier. They were concentrating on the east barrier, leaving the north barrier with no armed support.

Pushing the thought away, I ran headlong at the monsters trying to overrun my home. The first pikes found their targets as I carefully picked my way through the tripwires and punji sticks.

I cleared the obstacles and broke into a run. My path was immediately blocked by a heavily decayed body. That it was able to stand defied logic. My momentum carried me forward, giving me barely enough time to lower my shoulder before crashing into the beast. The impact sent the putrid carcass crashing to the ground, causing its guts to explode, splashing mucus and gore far and wide. Somehow I stayed on my feet. I brought my boot down hard on its head, ending the freak of nature's pilgrimage.

Lisa

The sounds of battle pulled Lisa to the picture window in the house she shared with Dillan. She was feeling better until she witnessed the chaos in the streets.

"What the f—!" She snapped her radio on and pulled a sharp breath when the chatter filled the speaker. In a controlled rage, she rushed to gear up and join the fight.

Hitting the street in full battle-rattle, she joined the flow of people heading to the east side of the community. Halfway there, she noticed Darline exit the community pantry and veered in her direction.

"DARLINE! What the hell's happening?"

Darline's panicked response pushed Lisa to her breaking point. "Thousands of UCs are swarming the barrier, and we're being sniped."

Darline's radio slipped from her grasp, causing both women to kneel to retrieve it. Suddenly, shards of wood exploded from the house behind them. They slammed flat to the ground and rolled behind the trunk of a massive oak tree.

Darline looked at the hole and realized the sniper had had her in his crosshairs. A fortunate accident had saved her life!

Lisa howled, "Oh, bullshit! No one does this to us." She struggled to a kneeling position and eased her head around the oak's trunk. When nothing happened, she sprang to her feet and yelled to Darline, "Find a rifle. I'll meet you at the barrier."

Ice filled Lisa's heart when she reached the battleground. People were taking cover anyplace they could. Pikes lay scattered near the fence with the body of a pike team member sprawled face down at its base.

Armed men and women knelt atop the catwalk, the barrels of their rifles flung over the barrier, shooting blindly into the horde. She watched in horror as most of their rounds ripped into the ground, missing their targets.

Red filled her vision while fury drove her forward. When she reached the cyclone fencing, she stuck the barrel of her Sig-MPX through a link and unleashed hell on the dead.

Randy

Furious with Otto, Randy stuffed his radio into his MOLLE vest. "He's trying to get himself killed!" he barked.

Nila entered the living room with Randy's prized, rarely used Colt SP1 pre-ban. "Who are you talking to?"

Randy gawked wide-eyed at the Colt. "Otto, he's outside the barrier." After a brief pause, he continued, "Can you, maybe, use the Daniel Defense? It's on the dining room table." He reached out and carefully removed the Colt from Nila's grasp. *She does not understand your worth. Back to the gun safe you go.*

Rolling her eyes, Nila stomped to the dining room and retrieved the freshly cleaned Daniel Defense AR. She slammed a full mag into the well, released the bolt, and moved towards the door. Randy stopped her. "I need your help. Grab the tripod."

Within minutes, Randy and Nila were racing towards the Southeast Tower. The M2 bounced around the back of Randy's truck while he developed a plan that wouldn't get them killed. At seventy-eight pounds, carrying the machine gun up the guard tower ladder using only his left hand would be impossible. He had removed his right arm from the immobilizer, but it remained too banged up to carry that much weight.

"I got it!" he exclaimed. "Park behind the dirt section of the barrier at its tip. I'll use the truck's roof as a firing platform.

Nila course-corrected and stomped on the accelerator, pushing the truck to its limits. With their destination in sight, the front of the vehicle suddenly pitched down and hard to the right. Nila struggled to maintain control of the enormous GMC 3500. Realizing that her efforts were failing, she stood on the brake pedal and prayed.

Smoke belched from the truck's wheels as it slid toward the packed-earth barrier. Panicked faces, trapped between being crushed by the truck or shot by the sniper, filled the windshield. Randy grabbed his door latch, preparing to leap from the cab, when the truck mercifully screeched to a halt inches from the barrier.

Randy checked on Nila, then immediately exited. The sounds of the dead stunned him. Their collective rasping nearly drowned out the sounds of combat raging mere feet away. He glanced at the front passenger tire; a large hole in the sidewall told him everything he needed to know. It had been shot!

Otto

The dead were focused on the mayhem erupting inside the community. I used their distraction to move through the throng of decay unnoticed. I fought the urge to draw my XDm. Shooting would draw their attention to an easy meal. Instead, I plowed through them like a fullback from the two-yard line.

I used every ounce of my one hundred eighty pounds to cut a path through their countless ranks. Twenty yards into my trek, I stumbled across a baseball-bat-sized tree branch and scooped it up.

Saturated in gore and quickly losing steam, I surveyed my surroundings. The UC horde seemed endless. *This was a terrible idea, Hammer!* I considered retreating to the safety of the barrier when the image of Devon's bleeding face filled my mind's eye. My refreshed anger pushed my doubts aside and I barreled into the crowd.

I moved against their flow, hoping to break free of the pack and circle around to attack the sniper on his rear flank. The tactic would give me the advantage of surprise and keep me out of our defenders' line of fire.

Panic took over when the mass shifted direction and began shambling towards me. I bounced and slid my way through the throng, but it was no use. They had found me. The UCs started bunching together, creating a tightly wound fabric of putrid flesh as they surrounded me.

With nothing left to lose, I spun the branch in my hand and charged their front line.

Eight Hundred Yards Away

Bobby's crosshair rested on the woman's forehead. He took up the pre-travel in the Dragunov's trigger, then quickly released it. Her violence fascinated him. Although he couldn't hear her, her mouth held the shape of a never-ending battle cry that would have frozen his troops in their tracks if they could feel fear.

"This one needs to die. Pull the trigger, Bobby. End her."

Bobby ignored Herbert's ramblings. Something about this woman captivated him. He began to envision the two of them running wild in the streets together, wreaking havoc upon the weak-minded citizens of RAM. He imagined how she would feel in his arms as she relented to his power.

"You are my soul mate," he whispered.

"She is your enemy. End her now before she destroys your entire army."

"Herbert, may I suggest you find a weapon and aid in my effort to suppress their resistance?"

Herbert's maniacal laughter grew faint as he retreated from Bobby's space.

"That's what I thought."

Bobby began devising a plan that would allow his soul mate to live and join him in his war against the people of RAM.

He wondered aloud, "What is your name? I shall call you ..." His thought shattered as a tall, slender man appeared next to Bobby's love interest, taking her face in his hands and kissing her passionately.

Bobby hissed through gritted teeth, "Whore! How could you betray me, betray us. What about our plans, our future?"

He turned from the scope and wiped the stinging tears from his eye. When the crosshairs once again found her head, he screamed, "Your life ends now."

Dillan

Dillan searched frantically for Lisa. He'd glimpsed her charging into battle but hadn't seen her since.

The sniper fire had paused, and the community's defenses began coming online. Gunfire erupted, seemingly from every inch of the community; pikes slid through rotten skulls, and the injured were finally tended to. They were fighting back!

His anxiety grew as he ran, searching the determined faces around him for the woman he loved.

Suddenly, a beautiful noise rose above the din of battle. Lisa's battle cry!

He followed her voice to the fence and saw her. Dillan bolted in her direction. He hadn't realized how deeply he cared for her until the thought of losing her entered his mind.

When he reached her, he took her face in his hands and kissed her as if it were their last. When he pulled away, she had a puzzled look on her face.

"What the hell are you doing?" she yelled. "We're in a fight. Move your ass, Slim."

"That's why I love you!" he screamed.

The rattle of a heavy machinegun startled them, prompting them to duck for cover. Dillan craned his neck, trying to identify who was shooting and who they were shooting at.

He was relieved to find Randy perched atop his truck, manning an M2 and shredding the UC masses.

His relief vanished when Lisa screamed.

Darline

Convinced she'd married the single most bullheaded human being alive, Darline knew what she needed to do. She holstered her Steyr L9-A1 and grabbed Otto's Ruger AR. She gave it a long, thoughtful stare. She wasn't as proficient with an AR as she was with her Steyr. But her plan didn't call for superior marksmanship.

Darline broke the thought and blasted from her home. Her legs pumped furiously through the chaotic streets. Her fear of losing her husband overrode her instinct to stop to aid the wounded.

Sweat poured from her face as she reached the barrier and scurried up the ladder. This section of the wall was manned only by the pike team. She found herself standing alone on the catwalk overlooking the wasteland outside their home.

Terror gripped her when the landscape came into view. The area was thick with UCs struggling to defeat the defensive barriers keeping them from the human meat just out of reach. Dozens of them struggled to free themselves from impalement while their brethren trampled their shattered bodies.

Pulling her eyes from the ghastly sight, she searched frantically for Otto. Darline found only more and more dead.

Yelling to the pike team, she asked, "Where is he? Have you seen him?"

Knowing who she was talking about but offering no help, one of them replied, "No, most of us just arrived." The terrified young woman continued, "We've radioed for armed backup. We won't be able to stop them if they reach the fence."

Darline understood what she needed to do. *Adapt and overcome*. She pulled the Ruger tight to her shoulder and opened fire.

Otto

Holding the tree branch horizontally in a two-handed grip, I crashed into the leading edge of the mass of tangled UCs. Gore splashed over my body when the most decayed monsters exploded like flies on a windshield.

I spun, trying to find a path to safety. No matter the direction, the scene was the same. Rotten mouths clattered for my flesh.

I wasn't ready to die, to succumb to the horde. The thought of being devoured sent me into a frenzy. I swung the tree limb like a madman, hurling insults and crushing skulls until its blood-slicked bark slipped from my grasp.

I yanked my XDm from its holster and stroked the trigger over and over. I needn't aim as the area was so crowded. Every round found dead flesh. My actions bought me ten precious seconds to regroup. A narrow way opened.

I brought my pistol up and sent a round into the closest UC when my slide locked back. *No time to reload, Hammer. RUN!* My thought pushed me forward through the rapidly disappearing path.

There it was. Open ground, virtually free of the dead. Hope spurred me forward. I had a chance!

Confusion suddenly replaced my hope when gunfire exploded behind me. Had our attackers mixed foot soldiers in with the dead to mop up the living?

I screamed, "Not today!" and pivoted to face my human attackers just as the forehead of a UC exploded. A blistering-hot object screamed past my right ear and cleared away my confusion. Someone had just saved my life!

I wiped brains from my face and glanced back to the barrier.

Darline stood tall with my Ruger tucked in her shoulder. My wife's a badass.

Eight Hundred Yards Away

Wood splinters pelted Bobby's face as he pulled the trigger to end the life of his soul mate.

They had found him!

He slammed to the floor as the heavy rounds strafed the house. He rolled to the door and shimmied into the hallway.

"It's too soon. My army still needs me." Suddenly, he realized his gun remained perched in the window. He dared a look into the room. The sight stung his only eye. His beloved Dragunov had been obliterated.

"You haven't beaten me. My army is great and powerful. You will lose."

Bobby searched for answers, a way to save his troops from inevitable slaughter. With a sickly wet smile, Bobby slid his hand along his dagger's sheath and prepared for his last stand.

Pat and Jackson

Pat stormed from her home. She had been caring for several of the community's wounded but could no longer sit idly by while a war raged outside.

She marched down her driveway and hailed Jackson on the radio. "Jackson Hammer, prepare that truck you've been working on. This bullshit ends RIGHT NOW!"

"I'm ready to go, Pat. Meet me at the main gate in two."

Jackson had just finished working on the enormous vehicle. He'd remained unaware of the attack until Natasha cut the arc welders' power supply. In a state of absolute panic, she filled him in on what she'd heard on the radio. Pat had radioed him soon after.

Jackson knew what he needed to do. He smiled because the International 4300 was going to war.

The truck's cab was now encased in rebar and heavy sheet metal. The cobbled-together armor plating protruded eight inches from the cab. Its windows were reinforced with chicken wire, while thick steel plates were welded to its undercarriage. It was ready for battle.

Jackson approached the gates as Pat berated a guard who apparently moved too slowly when given orders.

After the first set of gates opened, Jackson pulled into the secured holding area. Pat joined him in the cab, locking him with a hard stare and nodded her approval.

He signaled the guards to open the primary gate and revved the powerful diesel engine. When the gate fully retracted, Jackson slammed the truck into gear, released the clutch pedal, and blasted into the monsters surrounding the gate.

Dillan

Dillan turned back to find Lisa facedown and unmoving on the muddy earth. He latched on to the pull handle of her tactical vest, dragging her to cover behind Randy's truck. His heart stopped when he rolled her over and found blood soaking her vest.

Her eyes fluttered open and went wide with shock. She tried to sit up, but Dillan placed a hand on her chest, begging her to remain still.

"Why am I lying on the ground, Dillan?"

"Relax, babe. We need to get you to Sabrina and Durrell. They'll slap a few stitches in you, and you'll be fighting again in no time."

Lisa's eyes went squinty. "Bullshit. You're lying. What's going on? Try telling the truth this time!"

Dillan ran his hand through his hair, struggling to remain calm. "Baby, you've been shot."

Bobby

Bobby duck-walked to the stairs. The second story of his headquarters was being ripped apart by the heavy machinegun. He needed to keep his head low lest it be torn from his body. *"You failed again, Bobby Smith. What's it feel like to never have accomplished anything? Your entire life is a blooper real. A never-ending loop of failure."*

"Herbert, pay close attention to what happens next. You will witness greatness. You will witness what true bravery looks like."

Bobby's eye burnt wild with anticipation. His action would allow his troops to easily overrun the Right America dolts.

He scooched down the stairs on his butt, presenting the smallest target possible. Halfway to the first level, he scrambled to his feet and leaped the rest of the way. He was a hero to his soldiers, and he was about to prove why.

Otto

I had room for one thought in my exhausted head. *Son-of-a-bitch was that a long run.* I mean, I'm in decent shape for an old man, but holy hell! I needed to catch my breath before pushing forward on my *heroic* quest, which, by the way, no longer seemed like a good idea or very heroic.

My target stood less than fifty yards in front of me. What awaited me was unknown. Home was eight hundred yards behind me, and I knew what awaited me there. It was the reason I was standing here, the reason I was saturated with gore, and it fueled a fresh wave of wrath in my soul.

I no longer questioned my actions or doubted myself. I simply moved forward. Slowly at first, my pace quickened with each step to a jog, then a run.

I screamed for my home, for its people, for its dead. I screamed at the loss, the betrayal, and our failures. But mostly, I screamed for the ones in the house. I wanted them to hear their demise approaching. Fill their last seconds on earth with a terror known only to those who witnessed death stalking them like prey, forcing them to succumb to hopelessness.

Eight Hundred Yards Away

Bobby landed on the first floor, catlike and coiled to strike. The screams of a madman sent his pulse racing. He embraced the chaos of the approaching battle, allowing it to take control, to guide his actions. Adrenalin pumped through him as he awaited the opposing troops to invade his realm. In a low growl, he said, "You best have brought an army to this fight."

The door exploded inward, torn from its hinges. When the dust settled, one man stood alone in the shadowy opening.

Bobby sneered at the insult. "Only one of you? Do you know who I am?"

Otto stepped into the house, leaving the shadows behind, and answered, "I really don't give a shit."

When the man's face came into focus, Bobby went stiff. "It's you! They sent an old man ..." A distant memory stopped Bobby cold. He knew this man.

Otto moved closer to the one-eyed boy. Tilting his head, he said, "I know you, don't I?" A cheap grin broke on his face, and he continued, "Now I remember you! Sorry, I just didn't recognize you standing up, Long John."

The man's barb sank deep into Bobby's psyche, tearing open a scar so deep it threatened to bleed him dry.

Otto moved closer to the damaged man. He flexed his hands, preparing to fight. The images from the destruction of his home played in his mind. Otto's initial restraint allowed him to determine if his opponent was armed and alone. He wasn't armed; he was alone.

Otto struck. He closed the distance and landed an undisputed right hook to Bobby's jaw, sending him stumbling backward. He landed another bone-crushing blow, then another and yet another. Months of pent up hostility coursed through his body, focusing its violent release on Bobby's face.

The skin above Bobby's eyes broke open, filling his only functioning eye with blood. Blinded, he flailed his fists harmlessly. Otto blocked Bobby's feeble counter-attack, stepped in close, and slammed him to the floor.

Bobby

"This is your plan? Allow an old man to beat you senseless? You're a worthless failure. I hope he throws your broken body in the trash like your mother did!"

Bobby gasped for air. He rolled to his side then was suddenly yanked to his feet, only to be slammed back to the floor. He felt like a rag doll discarded by an angry child.

Bobby's mind clouded, slipping from consciousness. Again he got pulled to his feet, then slammed to the floor, once more to his feet.

"Fight back, you imbecile! You pathetic, insignificant piece of trash!"

"SHUT UP!"

Otto

I expected him to call me names, insult my manhood, maybe even spit on me. I didn't expect to be told to shut up, mostly because I wasn't talking.

His action set alarms off in my head. Was he talking to a hidden accomplice? Was it code for a dozen troops to storm in and rip me apart?

I released my grip, and he crumpled at my feet. My hand resting on my holstered XDm, I turned slowly around the room. The area offered no obvious hiding places, no nooks or crannies to facilitate a surprise attack.

Bobby

"Listen to me. Your troops on the frontline are talking. They think you're feeble. A wretched excuse for a leader. They're dying by the hundreds. Torn apart by the guns you promised to silence."

"If you don't shut your mouth, I will rip your jaw from your face and feed it to my men."

Herbert's skull-splitting laughter filled the room, his mockery igniting a fire in Bobby's gut.

Otto

My back turned to the bloody husk of a man, I barked, "Who the hell are you talking to? You're freaking me out, so clamp it."

I spun around to find the little maggot struggling to stand. "I admire your stick-to-it-iveness. But you're making a mistake."

I watched him wage war with gravity before continuing, "Okay, but death by old man is an embarrassing way to die." He remained silent. Now standing bent slightly forward, he stepped towards me. Bloody bubbles formed over his mouth as his breath came heavy and fast.

Bobby

Bobby leaped at the old man, but his foe anticipated the move. The man held his ground until the last possible moment before moving sharply to his right. Bobby twisted, trying to latch onto his enemy, but he remained inches from his grasp. Too late to right himself, he landed hard on his side. The sound of snapping bones reverberated through the tight confines. His ribs!

Bobby tried to scream but could not catch his breath. He thrashed wildly, struggling to pull air into his lungs. Suddenly he found himself staring into the old man's burning eyes. Jerked to his feet, he braced to be smashed back to the floor.

Through gritted teeth, the old man growled, "Your trial has ended, the verdict is in. Guilty as charged. Sentence: Death."

His head slammed against drywall, then to the floor. His mind sputtered, shutting down parts of his body as it answered death's call.

"You didn't even fight back. An old man has beaten you!"

Coughing out bloody mucus, Bobby's eye snapped open. He raked air into wheezing lungs and found Herbert standing in front of him.

"Where have you been? I've needed your help for so long."

"I've never left you. My help comes to you, but you refuse to see it."

Herbert's face twisted and stretched, his voice warped in and out. Bobby strained to hear, to receive the man's wisdom.

A whirlpool filled his vision, then clicked to clarity. He smiled.

Otto

"What the hell was that? Seriously, I need to know."

Long John didn't answer. He had just held a conversation with ... himself, in two different voices.

His un-patched eye searched the room, then focused on something behind me. He smiled and said, "Now, Herbert!"

I tossed him to the floor, pivoted, and found an empty room.

His scream brought understanding; I had fallen for his ploy.

Heart pounding, I spun back to face him. He charged, hand at his waist ... I hadn't noticed the knife. Until now.

They

They wait. Hungry and desperate to feed, they wait. They watch the mindless fall. Their time will come soon, but for now, they wait.

*

Continued in

Eternal Vigilance
The Divided America Zombie Apocalypse

To be released in 2021

Thanks for reading! I'd like to thank all of my friends and family for their support. And a special thanks to Heidi, Darline, Charley, Russ, and you, the reader! Without you, none of this is possible.

Reviews are valuable to independent writers. Please consider leaving yours where you purchased this book.

Feel free to like me on Facebook at B.D. Lutz/Author Page. You'll be the first notified of specials and new releases. You can email me at: CLELUTZ11@gmail.com

Life makes only one promise, to be challenging. So, rest if you must, but don't you ever quit!

ABOUT THE AUTHOR

Hello! I'm supposed to tell you a little about myself, so here we go. I bet you can't wait! I was born in Cleveland Ohio. I now live in NEO (North East Ohio) with my wonderful wife (she told me to say that). Our beautiful daughter lives in California with her extraordinary husband, and we miss them every day.

In my early adult life I spent time as a Repo-Man for a rent to own furniture company, a bill collector and heavy drinker. Then, I pulled myself together and spent twenty-seven years working my way through sales management in corporate America. However, one day, I was sitting in a meeting and the right person said the right thing at the right time and I realized enough was truly enough. I've always wanted to do this, write a book, and I realized that we, you and me, have about fifteen minutes on the face of this planet and I needed to do one of the things I had always wanted to do. And, well, this is it.

If you're wondering, yes, I'm a conservative, I own guns, and I hate paying taxes.

My hope is that one day you're sitting in a meeting, delivering a package, serving someone dinner, or doing whatever it is you do for a living and decide that enough is enough. It's the scariest thing you'll ever do. But I promise at no point in your life will you feel more alive than the day you take control of the life you're living!